CROSS OVERS

Other Books by Edward Allen Karr

SERIES: Socrates Lewis Stories
(Psychological/Religious Fiction)

Crosswinds – Book One

*   *   *   *   *

SERIES: Fringes Of Infinity
(Contemporary Fantasy Fiction)

Lin Finity and her Mayhem Rising – Book One
Lin Finity in Holding On – A Novella
Lin Finity and the Words Unspoken – Book Two
Lin Finity and the Islands of Time – Book Three
Lin Finity and the Flights to Forever – Book Four
Tayo Tersoo and the Hunter of Souls – Book Five

*   *   *   *   *

SERIES: Thrills N Kills in The Hills
(Racy, Comical Horror in Beverly Hills)

Dayzee Dazzle and the Kildare Killers – Book One
Dayzee Dazzle and her Manic Mansion – Book Two
Dayzee Dazzle and the On-Set Onslaught – Book Three
Dayzee Dazzle and the Cadaver Collectors – Book Four

*   *   *   *   *

SERIES: A World So Close
(Middle-grade Fantasy Adventure & Coming of Age)

Jayden Blue and the Gift to Imagine – A Prequel
Jayden Blue and the Sword in his Shadow – Book One
Jayden Blue and the Call of the Wings – Book Two
Jayden Blue and the Lair of the Iron Lions – Book Three
Jayden Blue and the Journey to Val ka'Yoom – Book Four
Jayden Blue and the Forest of Night Fallen – Book Five
Jayden Blue and the Wait of the Sun – Book Six

*   *   *   *   *

CROSS OVERS

Socrates Lewis Stories Book Two

Edward Allen Karr

LAKESIDE LETTERS, LLC

Lakeside Letters, LLC
30628 Detroit Road, #247
Westlake, OH 44145

Crossovers – Socrates Lewis Stories Book Two
©2024 Edward Sechkar.   All rights reserved.

First Edition, 2024
Lakeside Letters, LLC

Cover design by JD Smith Design

ISBN-13: 978-1-950886-63-0

Author's Note

I don't believe that Mara (still not her real name) had intentionally meant to mislead me about the timing of manuscripts produced by Socrates Lewis. So, I'll accept as truth her claim that she only wished, that second time that we'd met on a frozen Central Park bench, to keep his sequel manuscript locked away so as to make a free-standing publication out of his first manuscript.

Otherwise, she told me, Miley wouldn't get what one might call "just about the lead role" as she deserved.

As I learned from Mara just after *Crosswinds* was published, that whole endeavor of Socrates doing some investigative work on the "curious story" assignment that she'd given him hadn't yet happened. The focus of his life got pulled into something much juicier, a narrative worthy of its own book of storytelling truth fleshed out with storytelling make believe.

Unlike the first manuscript from Socrates, for this one, he didn't provide a clear title. So, that's on me. I hope he likes it.

As I did for his first manuscript, I sought to weave all of his factual recollections for that momentous day, not long after he saw Miley die, with amusing characterizations and intriguing plot points.

Mara, for one, wasn't completely amused by my fabrications of her off-color office escapades. But she grinned when she told me that, so perhaps it served as some kind of suggestion for her. Fiction can do that, you know: make something up (in our minds or in print), then we realize that we kind of like it, then we go make it happen.

Or try, at least.

Anyway, I've been told that Socrates will get busy with that investigation soon. Or he might have already trudged through that,

whiskey-free like Mara wanted, or whiskey-imbibed, which I'd prefer
for him. He seems to do his best work when the gears and
mechanisms of his mind are oiled just right.

But it's also possible that he hasn't given that project the slightest
consideration. He might be too ensnared in a trap too delightful to
pass up. We shall see.

Here, then, is the story of a day in the life of Socrates Lewis, in
the form of a novel and with the title *Crossovers*.

He would recommend a persistent sampling of whiskey, of
whatever brand, to accompany the turning of every page.

In fact, he told me so.

And I'd never dream of debating with an ancient philosopher.

~ Edward Allen Karr

Excerpt

From Chapter 9 – Bit of a Romantic

"Better run along, Mr. Philosopher. Who knows what might happen if you don't?"

He softly snorted out a breath and hurried back to the open doorway.

"Uh, okay, text me sometime, alright?"

Before answering, Aspin sat on the couch, gave a ballerina a crank, then set it down to play.

Then, she locked her blue eyes on his.

"I will."

Socrates tipped his hat, while holding his breath, and stepped into the hallway and closed the door behind him.

Then, he leaned his back into the door and listened to one of Miley's sweet melodies until it reached its end.

Table of Contents

Author's Note v

Excerpt vii

Chapter 1 – Miss You, Miley 1

Chapter 2 – The Hallway Too? 8

Chapter 3 – A Damn Nice Illusion 13

Chapter 4 – Math Hates Me 20

Chapter 5 – Your Addled Imagination 24

Chapter 6 – Does She Have Blue Eyes? 28

Chapter 7 – She Hooked You 35

Chapter 8 – I'm…Something Else 43

Chapter 9 – Bit of a Romantic 50

Chapter 10 – I Needed His Name 58

Chapter 11 – Very Much Like a Hooker 63

Chapter 12 – She Isn't a Philosopher 73

Chapter 13 – There. Feel Safer? 77

Chapter 14 – Jesus. Your Answers… 85

Chapter 15 – You Want to Pretend 89

Chapter 16 – Disguising Himself in Light 97

Chapter 17 – Something to Dream About 103

Chapter 18 – Where You Saw Her Die 107

Chapter 19 – You Rested Enough, Mr. Lewis! 113

Chapter 20 – Both…Of Them 120

Chapter 21 – Kiss a Goddamn Bus 125

Chapter 22 – Charging in with an Axe 129

Chapter 23 – I Look Sexy as Hell...133

Chapter 24 – She Pointed at Socrates...136

Chapter 25 – The Hellish Purple Ice Broke.................................140

Chapter 26 – I Should Just Laugh?...146

Chapter 27 – I Still Don't Know 152

Chapter 28 – Not Always Somebody's Fault.................................154

Chapter 29 – Starting It All Over 157

Chapter 1 – Miss You, Miley

He rubbed at his right eye, then his left. He blinked them both a few times. Still half asleep, he couldn't fight the satisfied smile that began a gradual arrival at seeing the white shoestring tracing a straight line down his reflected face, evenly dividing his forehead, along his nose, then halving his growing smile before keeping the sides of his chin neatly separated.

"God, what a relief."

Still holding his own steady gaze in the mirror above his dresser, he pointed to himself and said, "God. Not Jesus. It's only fair."

He allowed his eyes to trace down along the string until he saw the sparkling engagement ring knotted at the bottom. It spun slowly first one way, then changed directions. Each facet of the single stone caught a bit of the morning light coming through his bedroom window, sending him quick flashes as if poking him, telling him to get fully awake.

Socrates Lewis realized that he was counting those flashes, tallying the totals for each direction of the ring's spinning, before laughing softly and trying to ignore those tiny glints also bouncing off of the whiskey bottle and an empty glass.

After stopping himself abruptly, he turned enough to see the small window above his nightstand.

"Huh."

He grabbed a sock off of a pile on the dresser top, walked over, and gave a half-hearted effort at smearing around at all of the smudges that he'd never noticed through the days of rain and gloom that had threatened to never end.

Leaning, he looked out at the staggered walls of brick which sheltered neighbors that he'd never met, though some of them had proven their existence from time to time by staring back at him, sometimes even waving.

Others had sent him more creative gestures across the alley.

Up above the cornices of some, crumbling parapets of others, and the various vent stacks and chimneys of all, an unfamiliar flaring in the sky signaled an actual sunrise occurring, though Socrates knew that he would never see even a smidgen of it from his room.

He snapped to attention at the alarm clock close to his face proclaiming that it was 8:00 am and gave it a quick thump, convincing it to quiet down. Before moving his hand away, he grabbed the worn hardcover book lying next to it and held it up.

"Socrates."

Opening it to where a bookmark jutted out from the top, shiny and smooth and bragging about its relative youth compared to the book, he read the quote that had spoken to him all through the night: "Beauty is a short-lived tyranny."

The book got snapped shut, and he jerked the marker out and tossed it aside. After glaring at the cover for a moment, he dropped it with a thump.

Then, he nudged it around until it was in some sort of balanced alignment with the clock, then scoffed at the sight of it.

"God, if her beauty was a tyranny . . ."

Done with Socrates, the real one, he grabbed the window with both hands and slid it up, causing the curtains to immediately begin a fluttery dance from the warm breezes that he'd invited inside.

A quick couple of steps got him to again face the mirror and string and ring. He turned quickly toward the window, confirmed that the light winds were hitting him, buffeting him, trying to make him lean to his left like he had for so long.

But one eye looked back at him from each side of the white string.

"God, I really am done with that? No more leaning?"

Not waiting for an answer, he grabbed at the three pieces of tape holding the shoestring to the top middle of the mirror's frame, and he gave them a yank.

While pulling the tape from the string, he studied the residue still tacky and splotchy on the smooth wood. He hurried to finish scraping tape from the string, affixed the sticky pieces to the edge of the dresser, then reached for the muck left behind. But he stopped short, winced at the sight of it, then let his hand retreat.

"No. That's fine. Just like that."

Holding the string high enough to get the ring swinging near his eyes, Socrates laughed once, said, "Why not?" and fashioned it into a necklace, which he promptly dropped down over his head.

Clutching the ring with his left hand, he poured a full glass with his right, then held it up to toast his reflection.

"Miss you, Miley."

*   *   *

A feeble knocking was almost lost in Mara's dragging open one drawer after another as she engaged in an intensive search. She paused her efforts in time to be sure that the last knock was actually a knock.

"Come in."

The door to her small but orderly office where she acted as editor of the philosophy magazine, for which Socrates Lewis occasionally contributed, swung in slowly, and a young man with unruly black hair leaned into the opening, his eyes big.

"Martin, didn't I already tell you to come in?"

He grinned and said, "Not exactly. You told someone to come in. You didn't know it was me."

"I'm plagued by deep thinkers."

He kept grinning.

"Get your ass in here, will you? Jesus. I mean, um, gee whiz."

He stepped inside and coughed once, disguising his smile as he entered Mara's office.

"I, uh, know what you mean. That 'gee whiz' thing."

"Just forget that you ever read that piece by Socrates. I only wanted you to give it a quick read-through for a final check."

"We're really not publishing it, Mara?"

"No, we sure aren't. It's getting bloated out into a book of some sort titled *Crosswinds*. Let's just not mention it again, alright? I'd like to maintain some distance from that."

"Okay. Um, I just wanted to remind you that we're a little light on content for the next issue."

Her crossed arms lay on the desk as she leaned forward, holding his gaze.

"See? It all falls on me. Not much more than five years out of college, and the weight of the world is crushing my life into a soupy puddle already."

"It's, uh, it's kind of just a magazine that—"

"Oh, I know. I'm just reminding you of my superiority, that's all."

She leaned back in her seat, crossed her legs, and began an exam of her manicure. She wore painted-on jeans and sneakers, and her wavy brown hair lay strategically scattered on the shoulders of her tight sweater.

"Go ahead and give Socrates a buzz. I gave him an assignment the last time I saw him. Kind of an investigative piece. See where he's at."

"Call him?" he said, kicking at the floor with his eyes lowered. "He, um, he's always drunk."

"It does seem that way. But he's really—Martin, look at me."

He stopped toeing the area rug and looked back up at her.

"He's not always drunk. I suspect he sleeps through the night, which should flush some of his toxic wastes out."

Martin grinned and said, "Much better. He starts the day sober? That's what you mean?"

"Yes. I bet the drinking beats the sunrise, though."

She watched his eyes follow her legs as she crossed them the other way.

"You want me to call him, is that it, Martin?"

"Well, you're the getting-crushed editor, and you know him better, and—"

"Fine. Close the door."

He turned the knob and quietly shut it before letting the mechanism turn.

Before he could release it, she said, "Lock it."

He smiled and did as she'd instructed before turning toward her.

"You should be grateful that I'm providing you such a clear method for, um, rising up in this organization."

"I am, Mara. Thanks," he said, then continued while starting to take a step. "Each time we—"

"Stop."

He stopped.

"Verbal thanks won't get you far. Actions, Martin. Vigorous, tireless actions."

He smiled even as he started watching her kicking her crossed leg rhythmically, the laces bouncing, making him stare.

"You start with the shoes while I see if our excellent writer slash alcoholic slash wannabe philosopher has accomplished anything yet."

She picked up the phone, then stopped to say, "No," when she saw Martin begin the few steps needed to tend to her footwear.

"You know better than that," she said, shaking her head.

He grinned and dropped to his hands and knees.

"You like degrading me," he said.

"You like it more."

*　*　*

With the blank sheet pinched by both hands, held up from its comfortable home—wound snugly around the platen in his typewriter—Socrates scoffed and let it drop.

While letting a deep breath seep out, he gave his glass another pour, capped the bottle, and pushed it across the table toward two identical tall plastic containers containing birdseed.

Tapping the bottle with his fingernails, he studied their levels and saw that the one on the left was slightly higher. He reached for it, stopped short, and wrapped his hand around the drink glass instead.

"Maddening. Shit like that."

He tipped the glass up for a couple of quick swallows, then traded it for some sheets of handwritten notes. Dragging a pointing finger left to right along most of the lines, he finished the first sheet and tipped it toward him to scan the second.

"This is nonsense. So what if there's some people out there that don't trust science?"

Looking again at the first sheet, he said, "God, I just can't stop talking to myself. Except when I'm drinking."

He laughed once, snatched up his glass, and was about to pour some between his lips when his cell phone rang and buzzed and rattled on the tabletop.

"God, what now?"

He held it up, saw that it was Mara calling, then completed the drink without any further delay.

He cleared his throat, then tapped the phone.

"God, Mara, it's only Wednesday. Don't I have until the end of the week?"

After a pause, he heard her giggle, then she said, "Oh, yeah, for that research thing. Sure."

Another pause. Another giggle.

"That's more of a long-term project. We still need you to write up something for the upcoming issue, Socrates."

"I could, but—"

He stopped at the sound of another giggle, and he heard Mara, muffled, say, "I want *you* to do it. I have to watch my nails."

Then, in a normal voice, she said, "But, what?"

"Um, is everything okay there?"

"It will be. I'm just, um, giving staff their assignments."

"Uh, yeah. Right."

"Just part of my job. Look, we're a little lean for the upcoming mag. Try to slap something together, alright?"

"Slap?"

"Just write something. Then, get going on that research, Mr. Ancient Philosopher."

"I'm not really ancient, and I'm not so sure I want to be an investigator, Mara. That sounds like—"

"Look, I read that last thing you wrote. All about Jesus. Way more about that Miley girl, though."

"Well, yeah, Miley was—"

"A hooker."

"Uh, she was more than that."

"Sure. Well, she did some research, too, didn't she? You owe it to her. Carry on that tradition, so to speak. Just give it a shot."

He heard a male voice in the background whisper, "That buckle is—"

Even the slap sounded muffled, then Mara whispered, "Hey! I'm on the phone!"

He held the phone away at the sound of Mara giggling for several seconds, then it went silent.

"Huh. Weird."

Holding up the glass to finish it, he paused long enough to give the waiting empty piece of paper a strong flick.

Then, he reached for the seed container on the right and began pouring some into the right pocket of his long, dark trench coat, which was folded neatly over the back of the only other chair at the table.

Chapter 2 – The Hallway Too?

Socrates stood in the open doorway to his apartment, looking back inside and checking that the pieces of his life that he'd put in some kind of order were indeed in order. Some areas were organized, but others were intentionally left as they'd happened.

A last glance at the kitchen table made him smile: the seed container on the right held more than its twin.

"Maddening," he said, then he adjusted his fedora and pulled the door closed behind him.

Then, rigor mortis got him.

His eyes became welded to the splattering of red, orange, and yellow shapes that seemed to be weaving under and over each other, evading his gaze. The background, if there was one—he'd never been able to focus past the dastardly pattern—kept itself hidden, offering up the nightmare challenge to him while lurking behind, claiming some kind of deniability.

"God, there's more of you each time."

Still holding the knob in one hand and the scribbled notes in the other, he placed his right foot as close to the middle of the hallway as he could.

He held his breath and looked to his right, then to his left, toward the stairway. Then, again to the right, all the while never taking his sights off of the carpet.

And the red shapes.

And the orange and yellow ones.

How many? he asked himself. How many to the right?

He forced himself to look to the end, which wasn't too far. A painting hanging on that wall dared him to look at it, but he didn't. He couldn't.

He was counting.

The second time gave him a different number than the first time.

The third time was the same as the first.

He winced, closing his eyes, and forced himself to breathe.

Again, he counted from below that colorful artwork to that one step that he'd planted in the hall's middle. He tallied them up two more times and got the same number for all three surveys.

A deep sigh was his only reward as he looked down, let go of the doorknob, and slowly took a step with his left. Left to right and back again he looked, knowing that it had to be quick.

Because once he'd started to walk, there could be no more hesitation. He could be erratic and sloppy until he got to the balcony, but not beyond that.

Over that second-floor railing, the cavernous lobby waited, well-lit, saturated with every possible color, and likely brimming with eyes, all focused on him.

Watching his every step.

Studying. Scrutinizing. Keeping score.

There was sure to be a pair of little girl eyes—Wendy. And a bright green pair for that cat of hers that she'd named Rae Cat.

He counted twice, got the same number, and breathed easier.

While swinging his right leg forward, he raced his eyes side to side, always conscious of keeping a steady, relaxed gait.

The two counts matched again, just in time, and he stepped with his right, knowing that when he placed that step, he'd be on display for every curious eye below, especially the ones that seemed to continually inhabit that burgundy couch.

The numbers didn't match, and there was no time for a third count. There could be no delay, so he choked back that failure and took the next step.

And the red, orange, and yellow globs tormented him, rolling away from his study of them, diving beneath each other, laughing at his inability to count them even once.

But he had to keep going. Onward, toward the stairs.

His heart pounded, taunting him to count its beats, too, and he held the notes flat in front of his face, blocking the carpeting to finish the walk to the stairs.

He held the rail, standing at the top, and allowed himself the time to calm from that new ordeal which had never plagued him before.

"God, that was ugly. Now, the hallway too?"

Before contemplating the carpet runners on all of the steps, the ones with pale purple circles of varying sizes, all lodged into a darker purple background, he blew out a single, deep breath and looked toward the couch.

At the sight of Wendy and Rae, he smiled and shook his head, and the girl's smile made it easy to forget his hallway fiasco.

But his eyes got anchored to the light purple circles on each and every step all the way down to the lobby floor. He'd never cared about them on the journey downward.

Only traveling up. That's how it had always been.

With a sharp grunt, he forced his eyes back to Wendy and waved rigidly, like a mechanized mockup of himself, as he bumped his hand along the railing and descended.

At the bottom, shoes safe on the clean tile floor, with no pressing need to count circles, calculate their areas, then sum those areas up on each side of each step placement, a heavy sigh rasped out slowly.

Then, with a smile of relief and the promise of the good company of Wendy and her cat, he began the short walk to the burgundy couch. On the way, he glanced up at all of the bright lights suspended from the high ceiling with chains.

* * *

Socrates fought to keep from smiling as he pointed at Wendy, who made no such effort. She giggled and kicked her legs as they mostly stuck straight out from the couch, keeping the long laces of her sneakers snapping. From the lights above, her orange sweatshirt seemed all the brighter.

"I know you," he said, pointing at her and prompting her to cover her smile with one hand.

He looked at the black cat lying pressed up against her, pointed, and said, "You? Oh, I guess I'm starting to know you."

"Hi, Mr. Lewis. I know you too! So does Rae Cat."

Standing near, holding his notes in one hand, wearing his long coat and fedora, Socrates shook his head at them and said, "You both should know me by now. Because I always pass through here to . . ."

He paused and waited with his head tipped to one side.

"Feed the birds!"

He patted his side pockets, which bulged out slightly.

"Correct. No bird seed for you, though."

"Uh-uh. Not for me. Not for Rae either."

"Say, is she still eating from two bowls?"

Wendy petted the cat and rubbed her ears, but Rae only stared up at Socrates.

"No, Mr. Lewis. We ran out of her old food. She just has new food now."

"Oh. Well, I hope she's happy with it."

Wendy shrugged and said, "I think she is."

"You don't know?"

Wendy shook her head and said, "She didn't say so."

"Oh. No, I don't suppose she will. Hey, Wendy, don't you ever go to school?"

She nodded and said, "Yeah."

She pointed up at the balcony and said, "At home."

"Oh, I see. You're homeschooled. Are you learning a lot?"

She shrugged and said, "I guess."

"What are you studying? What subjects?"

She shrugged again and said, "All kinds of stuff."

When Wendy looked down at the cat and started scratching around between her ears, Socrates took a moment to enjoy all of the colors present in the lobby: the wallpaper, the artwork, the furnishings, and even the attractive tiles of the floor.

"Okay, well, the birds are waiting."

She looked up and said, "How do you know?"

He stared at the pair of big eyes looking back at him.

"Uh, I guess I don't. I do believe they are, though."

"I bet they are too."

He tipped his hat to her, turned, and walked toward the door, where he paused before opening it to study his reflection.

He saw that he was standing straight up, which brought a smile, then he looked through the glass at a cheery, colorful city shaking off the last of the night's shadows.

Chapter 3 – A Damn Nice Illusion

"They're funny. They don't hardly move anymore."

The wheels of the food cart that the man was pushing, his hands in unraveling gloves without fingers, were getting in their last squeals as he coasted it to a stop.

A few more squeals would have prompted the pigeon community to take to the air instead of just bobbing their heads and looking annoyed.

"I don't know," said Socrates, pointing at the birds, "but maybe they'd like hotdogs for a change."

"I always do," said the man as he came to a stop, his hands still on the push bar. "I sometimes eat up most of my profits."

"Oh. An easy thing to do—probably unavoidable."

While steam seeped out through cracks around vat lids in several locations, the vendor fussed with his weathered dark blue top hat and leaned to stare at the pigeons who'd halted their pecking at seed to stare up at him.

"Here, this'll help," Socrates said, then scooped the last of the birdseed out of his pockets and scattered it farther out, away from cart wheels that would soon need to resume the journey.

He and his regular breakfast chef watched as the birds leisurely pecked around, then engaged in some slow, almost sarcastically slow, waddling out of the cart's path.

"Yeah, birds," said the man, "no hurry. It's still early."

"They do like their seed."

"Wouldn't do much for me," said the man. "Seed, I mean."

"Because it's all the same color?"

The man stared for a second, then laughed, tipping his head and tall hat back for a second.

"What? No. What kind of lame idea is that?"

"Oh, I just know someone very special that told me that. What's your reason?"

"Easy. It'd all get stuck in my teeth."

Standing close to Socrates and beside his steamy cargo, the man held a giant smile for him to study, revealing a consistent absence of every other tooth, top and bottom.

"Um . . . that—"

"That's a joke! Don't bother me any if you was to laugh."

Socrates laughed but only for a second or two.

"That's not from—"

"No, it's not from the hot dogs. I should have been eating them for every meal. Like you."

Still watching the birds, Socrates said, "It's only for breakfast."

"I appreciate your business. And that sunshine—should be a nice day."

He'd just generated a short grinding out of the wheels from his two-handed leaning on it, then Socrates said, "Hey, look at that."

He looked.

Pointing away from the bench, past the train tracks at the barren rubble that had replaced warehouses that had been torn down long before, Socrates said, "That sign. When did that get put up?"

"You got some good eyes on you, mister. I believe just today. Looks like it's finally about to change into something different over there."

"Huh. That should brighten the city even more. You notice all the colors in everything today?"

He looked around, reaching up under his hat to scratch lazily, then back at Socrates.

"Yeah. Like usual. Speaking of usual, you want your usual?"

"No, sir. I'd like two of the jumbos today."

"You got it. The usual fixings too?"

"Hell, double everything. I'm celebrating."

He said, "What?" while fishing around, setting up his order.

"Sunshine, for one. Enough with the damn rain. And any day I can cut back on talking to myself, that's a good day."

Still looking into his vats, chasing hotdogs around with tongs like it was some sort of carnival game, the man in the top hat said, "Ha. I talk to myself all the time."

Socrates leaned, trying to catch the man's eye, but he was too focused on the meal prep.

"I've never heard you talking to yourself."

He stopped, a hot dog snagged and steaming and dripping in the cool air.

Staring at Socrates, he said, "I, uh, I just did."

*　*　*

"I'm sitting up straight," he said to the pigeons milling around near his feet.

He took another bite of a jumbo hotdog and said, with a full mouth, "Imagine if you all flew crooked, huh? That would annoy the hell out of you."

He looked to his left, saw the blue of the top hat tipping with each step as the vendor steered his cart to the next park over, one reliably crowded.

The feathers of some of the birds got puffed around as a stiffer breeze from Socrates's right hit all of them.

"Huh. The wind."

He stood and gazed out at the wasteland beyond the tracks, letting the cool air buffet him from the right.

A check down to the right, then down to the left, confirmed that he wasn't leaning in any noticeable amount.

"Good," he told the birds, none of whom seemed interested.

Then, he quickly turned to look toward the right and saw a figure approaching, dressed all in black. The baggy clothing kept itself animated from the wind, and the fedora needed the constant help of one hand to keep it in place up top.

As the pedestrian drew nearer, Socrates turned his eyes back to the birds and his breakfast. He held one up for the next bite and stopped before chomping down on it when the walker took a seat to his right.

He looked over quickly and saw only the back of a black suit jacket, oddly lumpy around the shoulders, so he shuffled to the left from his seat in the middle.

The hotdog forgotten, he raised up a cup of coffee and almost spilled it when the individual spun around and rested against the bench's back, facing the tracks like he. He gave a glance to his right, but the hat brim was tipped, the head leaning enough to keep secret their identity.

He looked forward and lowered the cup, then set it on the bench between them. From an inside pocket, he brought out a thin flask, pried off the coffee lid, and poured some into it. The bottle, capped again, got stowed away, and he snapped the lid back in place.

Then, he froze at the sight of a graceful left hand, wearing a few modest rings, as it reached for his cup.

He knew that his head was shaking as the hand lifted the cup, hid it behind the hat's brim until the head and hat and cup all tipped back once, then set it back down.

And the sunshine's warmth fizzled and faded as a chill hiked up and down his spine when a soft, feminine, familiar voice said, "Ah, that's good. Best way to start a day."

He stared, trembling, as the mysterious visitor leaned back, letting the hat brim float up lazily, revealing first lips that were already smiling, then a nose, then eyes that smiled, too, as a heavy shiver rattled him around in his coat.

"Miley!"

*　*　*

She turned to face him, bending her left arm up to rest on the back, and did nothing but smile at him, looking from his eyes to his silent, quivering lips, then back to his eyes.

Then, with both hands, she lifted her hair up out of the jacket and fluffed it all over her back.

"Sure looks like it, huh?"

"You're here? You're really here again? How could—"

"Ooh," she said, curling her lips into a tight circle. "Such a scary mystery!"

"Yeah! I mean, no, you're not scary. You're just—"

Nodding, she said, "I'm not Miley. Scary, maybe, but not Miley."

"I, um, I—" he mumbled while reaching in for the bottle, but she easily stopped him with just a touch.

"Figure it out, Mr. Socrates. I'll give you a second."

His eyes marched up and down and all around every feature of her smiling face. There could be no doubt that it was Miley's face.

She gave him more than a second.

But his only progress was to begin shaking his head.

"No? Okay, let me help. There's this thing called twins. Ever hear of that?"

He found her eyes, which could have been Miley's eyes, and decided to stay with that.

"You're not Miley?"

She held out a hand, and he stared at it for a second before taking it. And he felt the softness and warmth of it before again looking into her eyes.

She gave his hand a relaxed shake and said, "I'm Aspin. Recognize the clothes?"

She tried to get her hand from his, and he didn't want to let it go.

"That bar?" he said. "That was you?"

"Yeah. I try—oops, 'tried'—to keep an eye on her. That girl was always courting some kind of calamity."

"That was . . ."

Aspin squinted at the sight of his eyes traveling all over her face as his lips fumbled around, beginning so many different words that couldn't fight their way out. Especially with his breath locked in tight.

She scoffed, giving him a quick chill because even that could have come from Miley, then said, "Don't start thinking I'm a hooker, too, Mr. Socrates."

He settled on her eyes again, seeing that they might have been even more blue than Miley's.

"I, uh, that doesn't matter. You're . . . you're really not—"

"No, I'm really not. I'll tell you what, though. I can shut my trap right now and not say another word. Then, you can believe I'm whoever the hell you want me to be."

He'd been watching every tiniest detail of her lips while she spoke. He lingered there until he was sure that she'd finished, then looked up into her eyes, which clearly showed that she was waiting for some kind of response.

"No. Uh, no, don't stop talking."

"That could be a damn nice illusion. You sure?"

He tipped his head to study her features better, not even aware that his lips had some intention of forming a word or two.

Looking into her eyes again, he said, "No. No, Aspin. I want you to talk. You'll still look like—"

"Aspin?"

He let out one semi-hysterical laugh and said, "Yeah. Yeah, you look like Aspin."

"Damn right."

She reached into a pocket, then threw some seed out for the birds.

They'd only begun finding the seeds, staggering and jabbing beaks around, before she kicked out one leg, her black boot coming close to the flock, and they scattered into the sky with a chorus of unhappy warbling.

* * *

Aspin watched them winging themselves away from seeds and hostile boots, but Socrates only watched her face. She'd seen enough of their antics and turned to him, then leaned her head to one side, tipping the wide brim.

"I'll admit it," she said. "I like the way you're looking at me. My sister really was something, wasn't she?"

"Oh my, yeah. You, uh, you look so much—"

"What's my name?"

After a second, he said, "Aspin?"

"You're not sure? Say it again."

"Aspin."

"Better," she said, grinning. "One more time?"

He laughed and said, "Aspin. You're Aspin. But goddamn it, you sure could be Miley."

When she dug around in a different coat pocket, he watched her hand until she held out a small paper. He looked up to see that she'd been waiting for him.

"Yeah, I sure as hell could. Here."

He took the paper.

"Call me. Let's meet sometime."

She stood and locked her hands on her hips.

"That's Aspin's number."

He unfolded it, didn't even try to focus on it, then looked back up.

"Or, the offer's still good: I can shut the hell up."

She smiled, turned and walked only two steps before stopping and giving him just a profile view.

And a chill.

"That way, it'll be Miley's number."

Chapter 4 – Math Hates Me

Socrates swiped his key, then pulled open the glass door to enter his apartment building's lobby. He laughed to himself when he reached up to brush rainwater off of the sleeves of his trench coat, found none, then looked back through the glass at the sunny morning outside.

Turning again, his eyes got pulled like gravity to the burgundy couch not ten steps from the door. Wendy was there, lost in a book, but Rae Cat's green eyes were locked onto him, unblinking, compelling him, in the way of a silent cat, to suspend blinking too.

He shook his head and looked around the room before going to see Wendy. Up above, bright lights, all hanging by themselves, teamed up to create a sky dotted with suns. The walls and floors and furnishings and decor overwhelmed with color, all of it baking in that eternal daylight.

Giving Rae Cat the courtesy of another brief glance, which was returned with a cool glare, he focused on Wendy and coughed before walking. She looked up, closed the book on her lap with one finger as a bookmark, and waved with her free hand.

"Hi, Mr. Lewis. Did you feed the birds?"

Still walking the last two steps, he said, "Yes, Wendy, I sure did. They're always hungry. And you know what?"

With big eyes, she said, "What?"

"They're quite happy with seed for every meal."

She scrunched up her eight-year-old face and shook her head.

"Not me! I had cereal for breakfast, and we have to go upstairs soon for school."

He looked at Rae, then back at Wendy.

"Rae Cat, too, Wendy?"

She giggled and said, "No, not her. She knows everything already."

"She does?"

Wendy nodded and said, "About how to be a cat. I think she knows it all."

"I think you're right. So, what subjects do you study?"

She shrugged and made a face.

"I don't know. All kinds of things."

He pointed at her lap and said, "What's that? A schoolbook?"

She looked at the cover, then turned it for him to see, making a sour face.

"Oh, math. Lovely."

"It's okay. My mom tries to make it fun. Do you like math, Mr. Lewis?"

He drew in a deep breath, held it, then, without thinking first, looked toward the very first step long enough to see its mad swarm of purple circles, most of them already sizing him up. And laughing.

Looking again at Wendy, he let the breath out and said, "Well, Wendy, I think so. But I'm almost certain that math hates me."

She giggled and shook her head.

"How could it hate you?"

He coughed and said, "Oh, I'm just trying to make you laugh. You go ahead and study everything your mom teaches you. It's all very good."

"Okay. I'll try."

"Time for me to get upstairs. I hope to see you again sometime soon."

He tipped his hat and began his walk toward the stairs, but he stopped when she said, "Mr. Lewis?"

"Yes, Wendy?"

"Do the stairs make you tired sometimes?"

He frowned, then wiped it off of his face quickly.

"Well, I don't think so. Why do you ask?"

"I don't know. Sometimes, it just looks like you're tired walking up them."

He stared at her and a second later, she shrugged.

"Wendy, no, I just, um . . ."

He gave the purple circles another peek and saw that they were ready for him.

"I, uh, just have lots of things on my mind, sometimes. That's all."

"Things to write about?"

"Yes, exactly. I'll see you soon, okay?"

"Okay. Rae too."

"Yes, Rae Cat too. Should I bring extra seed for you?"

She scrunched up her face and said, "No, Mr. Lewis. No thanks!"

"I didn't think so."

He tipped his hat again and walked to the staircase, his eyes narrowing and focusing on the first of them. Before reaching it, he'd already taken several deep breaths. And before placing that first step, trying to get the exact spot where an equal number of circles was on each side of his shoe, and the spot where all the areas of the circles on one side equaled the areas of circles on the other side, he latched his eyes onto the painting above the top of the stairs.

And he silently thanked whatever decorator had spiked the damn thing to the wall right there.

Staring at it, not looking down even once at the stair runners, he felt his breaths getting quicker and shallower with every step. He wavered, near the top, and grabbed the railing for support.

Groaning out a purposefully deeper breath, he forced his legs to move, eyes on the painting, knowing that girl eyes and cat eyes were probably watching him, looking for any slight sign of hesitation.

The final step up to the hallway needed another groan, and he supplied it while trying to appreciate the colors of the painting leading him up.

He made it and still held the railing, standing there to catch his breath but feeling like collapsing. A quick spin of his head rewarded him with a wave from Wendy, suggesting that maybe he'd faked his travels on that minefield well enough.

That cat, though. That beautiful little Rae Cat. Those sharp little green eyes saw everything.

The cat knew.

But she'd never tell anyone.

Waving nonstop to Wendy, Socrates rushed, almost running, until he was at his door.

And when that door had opened, he did collapse.

"God, I've earned some serious falling down."

Chapter 5 – Your Addled Imagination

He laughed softly to himself, lying facedown across the ragged doormat and with his feet still in the hall, at noticing that he'd covered the flask with one hand to protect it as the exhaustion had toppled him.

"Priorities," he said with a chuckle as he began the process of standing up.

He leaned out to look both directions in the hallway, saw no one, and didn't dare look down at the menacing quagmire churning on that carpet.

The door closed behind him as he leaned his back into it, and Socrates gave his apartment a look, nodding at it being drastically less dim than in recent times.

Through a doorway, in the kitchen, another menacing item—a blank sheet of paper—stared back at him.

"Is that the same sheet that I left there before?"

He started walking toward it, fishing out the flask, and said, with a sharp laugh, "Or are you its twin?"

The sheet didn't respond, so he set the flask near the bottle and draped his coat over the spare chair. The hat stayed on, and he barely slowed en route to his bedroom, where he placed himself square in front of the mirror on his dresser.

"Huh. Still not used to seeing that."

He reached into his shirt and pulled out the necklace, the engagement ring on a shoestring. A change of grip let him view it in the reflection before he tucked it back inside and returned to the kitchen.

Seated, staring at the blank sheet, he held and sipped repeatedly the tumbler being steadily drained of whiskey. Looking past the typewriter, he saw the seed containers waiting for the next feeding.

Not level, like he'd prefer.

But a sign that he was making an effort.

He leaned enough to reach into a pants pocket and retrieved the folded bit of paper with Aspin's number. He unfolded it enough that it could stand on its own, near the bottle, and he stared at the numbers.

"God, that's sloppy. Like she used the wrong hand. Huh."

Still reading the number, he fumbled around with his left hand until he found his phone, which he tapped mindlessly against the tabletop until it rang, giving his heart a quick shove.

He grinned at it before tapping it and holding it to an ear.

"Lynnie. I was just thinking about you."

"Well, that's a surprise. What about, exactly?"

He grimaced and tightened his grip on the glass.

"Uh, it's about a new writing topic that Mara suggested."

"Your editor, right?"

"Yeah. It's kind of a research project, too, in a way. And you know me. I'm not the best with—"

"You're hell with a typewriter, though."

He smiled at the sound of her laughing, even as he flipped around the blank sheet.

"Thanks. But you, uh, you kind of know your way around computers and searching for stuff, right?"

"Yeah, I guess. What's it about?"

"Uh, I haven't decided if I even want to pursue it, Lynnie. If I do, I can—"

"Okay, fine. You figure it out. Hey, I heard you talked with Mom."

"Yes, we had a nice chat."

"Did she mention your writing?"

"Well, yeah, she did. We agree that getting back into some kind of groove with that would be good."

"And then?"

He frowned at his glass, then started swirling around what was waiting to be finished off.

"Then?" he said.

"Never mind. Hey, you never said what you were doing with that engagement ring. You just said something cryptic like it has some use to you."

"Oh, nothing special. It's just, um, kind of like an ornamental sort of—"

His phone alerted him to another call waiting.

"Hey, Lynnie, there's a call coming in. It might be—"

"The hotdog guy. Yeah, I bet. Okay, catch you later."

He tapped it a couple of times, then held it to his ear as the glass approached to complete its mission.

"Mara. Twice in one day? I'm really in demand."

"Uh, if you mean that I like demanding things from you, then sure."

"It was just a—"

"One of your jokes. Sure. Look, Socrates, one thing not in your notes on that project: when you get started interviewing, you should—"

"Wait. Interviewing?"

"Look, do whatever it takes. This could be big. You've been looking for a heavy topic, right, philosopher? So, when you talk to them, leave the whiskey at home."

While tipping the nearly empty bottle to each side, sloshing it around, he said, "Easy enough. But what if I just happen to be coming back from the liquor store, and I just happen to—"

"You'll just happen to make other plans. See? That's a good example of me demanding things of you."

He sighed and left the bottle alone.

"Fine. No booze when visiting these freaks that—"

"Who said they were freaks? Shave off a few slices of your addled imagination and splatter them on the blank sheet that's probably been sitting somewhere for a long time."

Socrates gave the blank sheet a quiet smirk and shook his head.

"Oh, and don't forget to get me something sooner too. That other project can wait. Not forever, though. Write something up by the end of the week."

"I do have some ideas that—"

"Hey, how about something on that weird priest you mentioned in that last manuscript? Something philosophical about a guy like that, huh?"

"Uh, I think Miley would have known more about him. And she—"

"She's gone. I remember. Sorry, I probably shouldn't have brought up any of that."

"Yeah, she, uh . . ."

He realized that his eyes were locked on the clumsy numbers of Aspin's phone number.

"She's gone."

Chapter 6 – Does She Have Blue Eyes?

Socrates devoted a glaring string of seconds to watching the phone as it lay to the left of his typewriter.

"God, enough calls already. I have work to do."

He looked just long enough at the bottle to the right of the typewriter to get his hand positioned correctly, then he began tapping his nails against it, starting with the little finger and progressing through the rest.

Leaning in to listen, he gave it another round of taps, smirked, and lifted his hand up a slight amount.

Nodding and satisfied that he'd found the right place to produce just the right tones, based on the level of liquid, his eyes found the blank sheet.

Eyes stared, fingers tapped, and typewriter keys enjoyed their freedom to sit quietly, untouched, advertising letters that were available for constructing words.

By Socrates Lewis.

For his next literary masterpiece.

"I'm not writing about that damn priest."

The tempo of his tapping got a boost.

"Maybe about Val? It would be a sordid philosophical exposition, a full-circle narrative on destroying an engagement by patronizing a high-priced floozy, then, decades later, daring to pose that life-altering question again, risking untold ridicule and scorn."

With his left hand, he fished around, found the ring, and held it in a tight fist. The right hand, all on its own, cranked up the tap volume.

Still holding the ring, still tapping, a relieved smile began to sprout as his eyes scoured a direct path from a large, empty sheet of paper to a much smaller piece which had been empty at one time, no doubt, but now served as a reference for calling the identical twin sister of a hooker whom he'd watched die.

"I could write about Aspin, I suppose."

It felt like eyeballs twitching except that it was voluntary as he swept his gaze in a tight line each way, repeatedly, across Aspin's handwritten phone number.

Trying to find the exact middle, vertically, of the string of numbers.

Then, adding the digits and seeking the middle, number-wise.

His left hand found the phone.

"God, she said she'd pretend she was Miley. Huh."

The fingers stopped, also without his express command, and pulled his eyes over to assist with a generous pouring effort.

He forced both eyes to the filled glass, and both hands followed their lead. Hands lifting, eyes watching the whiskey while he tried to keep the surface calm, he brought it closer to make half of it disappear.

Looking over the top edge of the tumbler, he saw the blank sheet waiting patiently.

Or maybe it was laughing in a quiet way, without a single word at its disposal.

"Wendy. Wendy always seems to have good ideas."

He finished what whiskey remained and clinked the glass down next to the bottle.

"Sometimes even that Rae Cat of hers. Maybe they're on lunch break?"

He quickly poured some seed from each container into each trench coat pocket, hurried his arms into the sleeves, then dropped his fedora onto his head.

Halfway to the door, he stopped.

"God, Wendy has that mother of hers too."

He stepped back to the kitchen table, rummaged around until he found a pack of gum, then snickered as he unwrapped two pieces.

Back at the door, he looked around at his abode, noting actual colors instead of every miserable shade of gray like before.

"Huh."

* * *

He'd been holding his breath far longer than he could stand, one hand still trying to crush the knob of his closed apartment door, so he blew it out noisily and looked down.

The red, orange, and yellow shapes couldn't be shunned, he knew.

He had to face them. Accept their challenge.

And maybe die right there in the hallway at the hands of smirking, mocking shapes that were weaponized to—

"God, I'm not about to die from this!" he whispered, then he let go to stand straight up in the hallway's middle.

He turned his head halfway around, then stopped, not completing the necessary study of the tormenting shapes behind him.

"Probably."

Looking ahead, past the transition from wall to a balcony railing overlooking a lobby with a burgundy couch loaded with inquisitive eyes—if they were on a break from school—the flowing shapes and patterns, all mixing together in a tortuous dance, hit him like a blast from a grenade, buckling him, dropping him to his hands and knees.

Seeing for the first time a dire need for glasses like that damned priest had worn, with lenses too black to allow even a sliver of light to pass, he bolted his eyes shut and whispered, "Oh, God. Maybe this damn rug will kill me."

He crawled toward the stairs and with each step of his right hand, he first sent it out to gauge the distance to the wall. Plodding along, his feeler limb confirmed that he'd reached the railing.

And that meant eyes. Little girl eyes judging him from the couch.

And cat eyes. Bright green. Thinking God knows what.

He stood and looked over the railing, zeroing in on a burgundy target to help exclude those other colors, the ones grabbing at his feet.

Wendy was there, reading a book.

Rae Cat was there, too, casting a cold stare that appeared disinterested but was actually just a thin disguise, Socrates suspected, to mask the incessant analysis occupying her cat brain.

He waved to the cat, then sprinted to the top of the stairs, where he attached his eyes again to the couch.

And a girl that kept reading a book.

And a cat that existed only to stare.

At him. As he failed on hallway and stair.

He tried to step without looking down, slipped, and felt both shoes strike that tread at about the same time, and he couldn't fight the urge to look.

"Two feet at one time? Huh."

He didn't even try to count three sets of circles, estimate their areas, and see whether his clumsy descent had managed to apportion purple circles into three camps with any mathematical precision.

It just couldn't be done.

Not with two simultaneous steps.

Ignoring the couch, realizing that his life might hang—or tumble—in the balance, he hopped onto each step until the final hop placed him safely on the clean tile floor.

He heard the giggling before looking to confirm it.

And his smile sprung up just before he saw Wendy shaking from her laughter, both hands over her mouth as she bounced gently on the burgundy couch.

Rae Cat only stared.

* * *

He tucked his smile away for the moment and walked toward Wendy and Rae.

On the way, he pointed toward her and said, "I know you. You're that girl that sits on that couch."

She let her hands drop, one of them finding the cat's back, and she didn't stow her smile away anywhere.

"I know you too. You feed the birds!"

Standing near the couch, Socrates said, "Hello, Wendy. Lunch break?"

She shrugged and said, "Kind of. We already ate, though."

"Oh. That's good. Rae Cat too?"

Wendy nodded and continued petting the black cat.

"She likes her new food. We have to go back upstairs soon."

"Yeah, back to school."

She giggled a few times and said, "That was funny!"

"What's that?"

Grinning, she pointed toward the stairway. He started to look for himself but only grinned, too, and pointed at the girl.

"Glad you liked it. I do try to make you laugh sometimes."

"You did all that for me?"

"Uh . . . how much did you see?"

"I saw you hopping down the stairs."

"Yes. I did some fun hopping."

She looked up toward the balcony and said, "And you crawled up there."

He allowed himself to gaze up at the railing and the infernal patterns that lay in wait for him the next time he'd journey that way.

"I, um . . . oh, you know what that was?"

She shook her head and said, "Uh-uh. What?"

"I was thinking about Rae Cat, and I wondered what that railing looked like to her. She's always down low like that, on all fours."

"Oh. Like a cat."

"Yes, exactly, Wendy."

"What was it like?"

"Um . . . not much different. Kind of the same."

She nodded and focused for a while on the cat's ears. The cat focused continuously on Socrates's eyes.

He squinted at the green eyes that he couldn't recall had ever blinked and reached in for the ring, strung around his neck with a white shoestring which was no longer needed for balance and posture and such things.

"What's that?"

He looked down as he brought it out.

"Oh, this. It's a ring."

She laughed and shook her head.

"What?"

"Mr. Lewis, you're being funny again."

"I am?"

She nodded, still smiling.

"How?"

She pointed at his necklace and said, "A ring goes on a finger."

He laughed, too, and said, "Oh, you're very right, Wendy. This type of ring especially is meant to be given to someone to wear on her finger."

She looked puzzled.

"Then, what's it doing there?"

Socrates stared down at the child, who stared back at him.

So did the cat.

"You're very wise, Wendy. So is Rae Cat, probably, though she doesn't say much."

Wendy giggled.

"Yes, it truly does belong on someone's finger."

"Does she have blue eyes?"

"Oh, uh, you remember that, huh?"

Wendy nodded and kept petting the cat.

"Uh, no, actually, she doesn't. Still, blue eyes are quite nice."

With a very serious expression, Wendy said, "Rae has green eyes."

He knew that those green eyes were locked on him, but he looked to confirm it anyway.

"Green eyes are very nice too."

"Mr. Lewis?"

"Yes, Wendy?"

"I'd love Rae no matter what color her eyes were."

Socrates felt his lips fumbling around, unable to construct any specific word.

"Wouldn't you?"

"Yes, of course, Wendy. That's very wise of you. Again. I'm going back upstairs to make a call."

"You don't carry your phone around? My mom does."

"Most folks do, that's true. No, I'm not fond of unexpected ringing when I'm trying to, um . . ."

"Feed the birds?"

He laughed, looking down on the girl and her cat, then patted his coat's side pockets.

"That's where I was going. How did you know?"

She shrugged and held her eyebrows up high.

"Because you always do, Mr. Lewis."

Chapter 7 – She Hooked You

The painted metal of his door felt cool against his forehead. Smooth, too, as he pressed against it as if allowing some glue to set. So he could relax and just hang there awhile.

My hat, he thought. Shouldn't the brim of it be . . .

Focusing on his pained breathing, he forgot the fedora, remembering only the crazed dash he'd made up the steps, two at a time, stumbling once, then sprinting to his door.

All while holding his breath.

Trying like hell to not think of the little girl eyes and cat eyes, no matter what color they were.

"Oh. It's probably on the floor."

He tried fixing his gaze on the very top of the door while at the same time stooping down, reaching around behind him.

His neck didn't like that plan. It didn't snap anywhere, but he knew that it was about to, so he stood back up.

"God, one thing after another."

He turned the knob and squeezed himself through before it was open enough, then slammed it behind him.

His breaths didn't seem to want to calm down, but he insisted.

It took a few minutes.

Then, he got down on hands and knees—imitating the cat, again, he thought—sealed his eyes shut, then opened the door just wide enough to snake out an arm.

The snake snagged the hat and dragged it inside.

After installing it, he sat and leaned back against the wall next to the door, causing the brim to hit the wall and tip forward, dumping the hat in his lap.

"Well, I'm inside. That's the thing."

Before getting up, he slipped out the flask, found some encouragement to continue his day, and stood.

Looking into the kitchen, seeing a blank sheet in a typewriter with a whiskey bottle for company, he said, "What would I do without Wendy?"

* * *

"Lynnie, it's Dad. You busy?"

"Not too much. What's going on?"

Socrates was again stationed in a perfect location to type up something fantastic. Not a single letter had yet appeared in a sheet of paper gathering dust, but whiskey had been poured.

"I'm just thinking that I'll probably go ahead with that research thing that Mara dumped on me."

"She dumped it, huh?"

"Well. Figure of speech. So, you're acing your way through college, and you—"

"Thanks, Dad."

"You're welcome. You really are. You make us proud. So, you—"

She laughed and said, "The way you said 'us.' Kind of cool."

"Uh, your mother and I. Yeah."

"Hey, I can't wait any longer. Tell me what kind of value that old engagement ring has for you."

"Uh, well, I suppose I could . . ."

He listened to his silent phone for a few seconds.

"Well?" she finally said.

He winced and almost laughed at how that ring had become used to being locked in a fist, even while using the phone.

"I, uh, I used to keep it hanging up above my dresser. Just something to look at."

"Hanging? Alright. Sure. Why not just set it somewhere so you can gawk at it?"

"Well, Lynnie, I don't know that I said anything about—"

"Okay. No, you didn't say you gawked at it. But why hang the thing?"

He hesitated and squeezed the ring more tightly.

"Um, there was a very specific reason for it. It kind of helped with, uh . . ."

"Yeah?"

"How about if I tell you when I see you?"

Again, the phone kept quiet.

"Who said we were meeting?"

"Um, no one. Not yet. But we could both say it."

His right hand was loaded up and ready to drum out a swift rhythm on the whiskey bottle, but he held it tight like a claw.

"Okay," she said.

He tapped all four fingers. Just once through the rank.

"Sure, Dad. To talk about that research thing?"

"Yeah, Lynnie. And I'll tell you why I've kept that ring hanging."

"I am curious. Alright, you said you used to hang it up. What are you doing with it now?"

He wondered if his other hand, the one wrapped around both ring and phone and that had also become a rigid claw, could generate enough pressure to fracture a diamond. The phone, probably.

"I'm just sort of carrying it around with me."

"Dad. Really?"

"Yeah, Lynnie. It, uh, keeps it from getting stolen out of this place."

"Right. Uh-huh. Good plan."

"So, what do you think? You think you could stop by later?"

"Sure, Dad. Alright. I have some stuff going on, so how about if I text you later to see if you're available?"

"I kind of always am. Unless I'm—"
"Feeding the birds. I know!"

* * *

Still holding the ring, the phone minding its own business on the left side of the typewriter, Socrates took a moment to savor a series of slow sips from his glass.

He set it down but didn't let it go, then tapped it against the bottle a few times.

"God, how long has it been since I've seen her?"

He let go of the ring and the glass and picked up the phone, then tapped it a few times.

"What?"

"Mara, I—"

"I'm almost out the door for a much-deserved lunch break, Socrates. What do you want?"

He grabbed at his notes that he'd written while talking to her earlier about the assignment.

"This won't take long. I just—"

"It better not. I need some relaxed time to eat. We can't all choke down hotdogs and be on our way."

"You . . . you know about that?"

"Oh, come on. I think everybody does. Well? Get to the point."

"Okay, uh, I have notes from when you told me about that cult thing that's—"

"It's probably not a cult. Did I call it that?"

"Uh, no. No, I don't think so. Alright. So, I was wondering if you could give me any details on your contact?"

"The one that tipped me off to all that?"

"Yeah. That one."

"The one that has inside info and asked to remain anonymous?"

"Uh, I think you're about to say—"

"No. The answer's no."

"But I could—"

"No."

He turned his fingernails loose, filling the kitchen with a frenzy of tiny clicks, four quick, then a gap, then another four. Then, he wondered if he was subconsciously sending out a Morse Code message.

"Anything else?"

"No, I guess that's—"

"Go get another hotdog, Socrates."

"Oh no, I had those for—"

"And cut back on the whiskey. And write something. Can you handle all that?"

"Uh, yeah, I sure—"

"Good."

He held the phone out to stare at it, gave it an exaggerated smirk, and clanked it down to keep the comatose typewriter company.

* * *

Reaching for the depleted whiskey glass, Socrates bumped the scrap of paper that Aspin had given him. He pinched it and held it up, studying the numbers.

"What did Miley say? That I have a thing for hookers?"

He dropped the note to hold his phone instead, and he keyed in all of the numbers save the last one.

"Huh. I sure have a thing for Miley, now, too."

He tapped that last digit and waited. A few seconds later, Miley answered.

Or so it seemed.

"This is Aspin."

"You sure sound like Miley."

"Look like her, too, Mr. Socrates. Except for her short skirt and heels."

"She wasn't always a hooker, you know."

"Well, that would be kind of weird."

He noticed that his right hand had begun fishing the ring necklace out into the open, all on its own, and he tipped his eyes down to watch as it got positioned just right.

"That's what I told her."

"Great minds . . . and all that."

"I guess. Anyway, I'm just calling to—"

"Good decision. Let's start out where we first met."

"No, that's not what I meant. Hey, that could mean at that bar off the alley, right?"

"We met?"

"Uh . . . no. So, you meant the park."

"Bingo."

"Miley said that too. About something else, though."

"Sisters. What can I say?"

"Identical. Yeah."

"More so if shut my mouth, right?"

"Oh, I guess that—"

"You want me to stay quiet for you? You could believe whatever you want."

"I, uh, I probably could if—"

"Hey, I could even dress like her. Think about that."

He felt his whiskey glass, safe in his hand, trembling and dinging against the table and bottle. A few more seconds passed, and he found that trying to embed the glass in the wood surface didn't work, but it did keep the rattling to a minimum.

"Good. You thought about it."

"No. I mean, yeah, but I'm just calling to say that we probably—"

"Should go to Miley's apartment together. Yeah, I was thinking the same thing."

"Huh? You're serious?"

"Yep. Dead serious. Okay, bad choice of words. You know what I mean."

"That might not be the best—"

"You have any big regrets in your life?"

"I, um . . ."

"Passing on this could be your biggest. Want to take that chance?"

"I, uh, I only knew her for a short while, and she—"

"She hooked you. Hey, that's kind of funny."

He laughed, gave the ring a glance, and encouraged the whiskey glass to keep itself quiet.

"Yeah, that kind of is. Uh, well, she's—she was—pretty remarkable, but I think—"

"You think you'd like to get your ketchup and mustard stained fingers on her journal."

"Her notes? About all that crosswind stuff?"

"Yeah. I think she'd want you to have that. I figured she'd told you about that."

"Yeah, she did, but . . ."

He stared across the room and gave the edge of the glass a soft clunk on the table.

Then, another.

And his phone let the silence drag on.

"She did tell me about that."

"And? Keep going."

"And, I . . ."

"Yeah, Socrates?"

"Alright. I sure would like to have her notes."

"Thought so. Grab some seed and get down to that bench with your name on it."

"Um, I was about to—"

"The hotdogs and ketchup and mustard are on me."

He felt his lower lip twitch a few times, but he had no clue what words it might have had in its mind.

"Don't tell me you took that literally."

"Um . . ."

"You could, though."

He heard Miley's laugh through his phone.

"See you in a few minutes."

He felt the glass vibrating in his hand and congratulated himself on making sure that it contained very little liquid.

But he saw the phone in his hand shaking.

And he knew what would likely be simmering in his brain every time he again had a hotdog.

And ketchup and mustard.

Chapter 8 – I'm…Something Else

At the bottom of the stairs, feeling certain that he could hear all of the faded purple circles heckling him, Socrates stood and sweated in his trench coat, staring gratefully at a couch devoid of Wendy or Rae Cat.

Mostly, of their eyes.

The demented gymnastic sights they would have seen, he thought with a wry laugh.

He patted his side pockets, confirming the presence of birdseed cargo, then ambled weakly across the lobby's tile floor toward the door.

Adjusting the brim of his hat while looking through the glass at a sunlit street holding apart tall walls made of bricks, he allowed his eyes to focus on his reflection instead.

He started to grin at the sight of a man standing straight and tall, then his still-pounding heart reminded him that there were still a few personal issues that might need some attention.

Like carpet pieces on stairs.

Like predatory patterns inhabiting the hallway floor.

He held his reflected gaze, or close enough, not being sure exactly where the eyes were with so much glare from a lobby ceiling that seemed to be built of lights. And he knew that that carpeting and all that nonsense could be addressed anytime.

Memories of Miley were always poised to pounce when he least expected them.

Plans for Lynnie's mother, Valerie, and a ring against his chest, hanging from a shoestring, were demanding some final verdict.

Make the offer? Or wait another couple of decades?

"God."

And then, there was Aspin too.

Who looked exactly like Miley.

And who would soon be alone with him in Miley's apartment.

"God, I should have checked that book up there. I'm sure that ancient Socrates had all kinds of ideas about a situation like this."

He scoffed and pushed open the door, welcoming a warm breeze that had only recently had all of its rain wrung out of it.

*   *   *

He'd felt his heart relaxing as he walked toward his regular park, but it changed its mind at the sight of Aspin on the bench, crossing a leg wrapped in a stretched layer of black denim.

He watched her kicking a black high-heeled shoe as he drew near, and his eyes seemed content with that until he noticed her turn her head toward him, then brush back her hair.

Waving, he closed the distance and grinned at the deliberately cute wave she gave back.

"Have a seat," she said.

"Hi, Aspin, nice to see you," he said while sitting beside her as she occupied the middle of the bench, leaving him no choice but to sit close.

"You're sure?"

"Yeah, of course, it's good to—"

"No. Not that."

He turned enough to see her smile, which was Miley's smile that he'd seen too few times.

"Uh, no. I'm not sure. Not completely."

"You saw her die?"

He looked out across the railroad tracks, toward an abandoned area that contained a lone sign alleging that it would eventually find some level of renewal.

"Uh, yeah. A speeding bus took her out."

"You're sure?"

"God, yeah, it was speeding. Yeah, it was—"

"No. The bus."

"I kind of hate buses now."

"Not surprised," she said and joined him in studying the desolate landscape.

"Whiskey for breakfast is supposed to help with all that?"

He grinned and reached for his inside pocket.

"You're saying I should cut back on that. I see. More for you, then."

He handed her the flask, and she uncapped it for a long drink before handing it back. Then the cap.

"If you insist," he said, then drained some of it before stowing it away.

"I'm not that confused. You're just, well, you're identical. What do you expect?"

He turned toward her when she said, "I expect it to make you crazy."

Watching and waiting to see her laugh, or even smile, didn't pan out. So, he sighed and looked forward again.

"Uh, maybe I had a head start."

"You and everyone else."

"Miley asked me," he said, "when I first met her, if—"

"If you were already a madman. Are you?"

"How did—"

"Her notes. Curious what else she wrote about you?"

"Hell, yeah. Of course. Did she say anything about—"

"Liking you?"

"Jesus, what are you doing to me?"

"Are you asking me or Jesus?"

He searched for any trace of a smile, and he found something. A hint of one. But it faded before growing into itself.

"You. I don't talk to Jesus anymore."

"God, though."

"Yeah. Sometimes. I slipped up just now."

She threw some seeds on the walkway, drawing a few pigeons, which she watched pecking at it.

"You feed the birds a lot?"

She kept her eyes on the birds and said, "Never."

He stared at her for a second, then shoveled out heavy handfuls from each side pocket.

"Watch a professional," he said, then scattered it all over, inviting a squawking flock of them.

"Miley was a professional too," she said.

He turned to her, wondering if his new habit of twitching around his lips while saying nothing was being written into his DNA. She kept looking ahead.

Still studying her, he said, "She was more than that."

Aspin finally turned to him, smiled, and said, "It wasn't a test, but you passed it. Want to visit Miley's secret hideaway?"

"Yeah. Sure."

He watched her face take on a sharper cast, any trace of a smile banished.

"You don't sound sure. Are you fucking sure, Socrates?"

He felt a single, jagged chill scrape along his spine, and he saw Miley's face, as she stood on the sidewalk before she died, speaking the same way. Exactly the same way.

Focusing on Aspin's eyes again, his heart slowed some at the sight of her relaxing into an easy smile.

"Yeah, Aspin. I'm fucking sure."

* * *

They walked side by side along the rough brick walls, sometimes passing doorways and street vendors with the continuous company of cars and trucks rolling past and exhaust fumes cavorting with aromas from hot food. Though sunshine only occasionally clawed its way into the depths of the caverns, Socrates always saw colors, and all gloom had fled.

"She said something about you leaning."

He took a few more steps before answering.

"She wrote about that too?"

"Sure. Girl was a maniac for writing stuff down. All kinds of stuff."

"Even that? We only talked for a minute."

"Hey, I'm not a psychic."

"Uh, no, I didn't think so. Yeah, I did tell her about that."

"So, what's the deal?"

He gave her a glance, but she only looked ahead as they continued hiking toward Miley's apartment.

"I had this weird posture thing going on. I was almost always—"

"Leaning to the left. Yeah. Not anymore?"

"No. I think that's done. Thank God."

"Not Jesus?"

"Well, sure," he said. "Him too."

"Covering all the bases, huh?"

"Yep. I'd still be leaning if I'd never met her."

"She helped you fix that?"

"No, not like that. Just knowing her, that whole experience, helped."

She grabbed his arm, forcing him to stop then face her as people walked past them in both directions.

"I look just like her. You need anything else fixed?"

He snorted out a laugh and said, "Carpeting. Aspin, I need help with carpeting."

She grinned and pointed at his face.

"She did write that you might be a madman."

"I guess I kind of am."

She lost her smile and dropped her pointing finger.

"If you were mad for Miley, I get it. She was something."

He stared into her eyes, bright blue like Miley's, and felt himself about to drown in either one of them.

"Well," he said, still looking into her eyes, "with a face like hers . . . "

Aspin scoffed and shook her head.

But she struggled for a second to find a comeback, and she gave up. Instead, she took his hand and got him walking beside her.

Socrates held back his smile as he felt her hand, smooth and warm like Miley's, holding onto his.

*   *   *

"Here," she said.

Socrates raised his hand, the one still holding Aspin's, and pointed toward a building entrance a few steps ahead.

"That one?"

He didn't look where he pointed, instead looking at her hand holding his.

She didn't look ahead either.

"Does it look like hers?" she said.

He'd lowered their hands and was watching the entrance.

"How should I know? I've never been here."

He felt a firm squeeze of his hand and heard, "No. You weren't looking at that."

Socrates laughed and said, "You don't miss much, do you?"

He looked at her until she returned his gaze.

"Not a goddamn thing."

The door was within reach, so he pulled it open and when she went through, he tightened his grip and kept her hand.

*   *   *

"Up the stairs," she said, and tipped her head in that direction.

48

Walking up, they passed a sloppy older woman coming down, and she said, "Hi, Miley."

Aspin said, "Hey. How are you?"

Socrates was staring from one to the other, making no effort to keep his mouth closed.

"Good," said the woman. "See you."

"You too."

Aspin led the way up, still holding Socrates's hand, who looked behind them at the woman several times.

"Aspin, she—"

"She thinks I'm Miley. Yeah."

They got to the landing, and Socrates said, "But, you . . . you're—"

She stopped quickly and turned, and he almost collided with her, face to face.

"I'm . . . something else. How's that?"

She bounced her eyebrows up and held them for a second, not smiling, then turned and took him along with her toward Miley's door.

Chapter 9 – Bit of a Romantic

"Go ahead and knock," Aspin said, and she waited a few seconds before turning to Socrates with a smile.

He laughed but only once, too busy examining the red satin heart suspended from the doorknob with a delicate chain.

"Hey," she said while aiming a key for the knob, "why don't I sneak in there first and answer the door?"

Shaking his head, he gave her only a brief glance before looking again at the heart, prompting Aspin to look too.

"Just joking. No need to mess with your head quite that much."

She tapped the heart, got it swinging, and said, "Bit of a romantic, that one. Bet you didn't know."

"I . . . think I knew."

A moment passed, both of them watching Miley's decoration until it had come to a rest.

"That's just a hint. Brace yourself," she said, then turned the key, then the knob.

She swung in the door and swept her hand toward the interior, giving Socrates room to get past her. He took one step through the doorway and stopped.

Not speaking.

Moving only his head as his eyes led the way over everything he could see.

"Hey," she said, "let's get out of the hallway before someone else calls me Miley."

She laughed, but he didn't. He only took one step to the side, letting her in, and she closed the door quietly.

Miley's small living room area was clean and colorful, decorated expertly. The upholstered furniture all had throw pillows of various shapes, most with delicate lace fringes. The walls carried framed sketches of unicorns, fairies, and cartoon characters, all signed with only a letter "M."

She'd been watching his eyes and said, "No letter 'A' on any of those. That's all Miley."

He couldn't answer.

His eyes had become fixed on a music box on an end table beside the couch: a graceful ballerina with her arms out, her dance paused so that she could stare directly at him.

"I, uh . . ."

He looked toward the opposite end of the couch, and he held his breath at seeing another ballerina peeking above the couch's arm.

Her eyes were also locked on him.

"She must have known you were coming and set them up like that."

It took a while before he could speak.

"She, uh, how would—"

"Maybe I set them up for you."

He broke away from the far dancer to look at Aspin.

She smiled and said, "Who would know the difference?"

His lips were moving again, grasping for words or even just a first letter, but they failed as he stared at her in silence.

She grabbed his hand and said, "Just a peek," and led him to a doorway.

He stood outside Miley's bedroom and looked in, seeing first the orderly line of stuffed animals keeping guard in front of a row of small pillows, which were safeguarding the actual sleeping pillows.

With his breath becoming grating and strained, he looked lower and saw the crisp edges of the dust ruffle an exact even distance just above the shiny wood floor.

He leaned to scan the top surface of her dresser and wasn't surprised to see a collection of snow globes, some with their own ballerinas, others with pandas on tree trunks or birds in flight, many more providing watery worlds for hearts of every size and color.

When she said, "I lied," she got his attention.

"About what? Your name?"

She pointed at his face and smiled while saying, "You wish."

"No, you're Aspin. I accept that."

"I meant that maybe I do need to mess with you a lot."

He sighed and said, "You're good at it."

"Yep. Look around, Mr. Socrates. It's a side of Miley I don't think anyone else knew of. Just you, me, and her."

Looking around again, he said, "This is almost too much."

He reached in to hold the edge of the dresser, which was close, and wobbled without trying to take a step.

"Yeah. I bet. My room is nothing like this."

He let go to stand up straight and faced her, not asking but waiting for details.

"It's all wrought iron."

He tipped his head but didn't look away.

"And leather."

She pointed at him just once and said, "Black."

He'd started shaking his head, his breaths getting deeper, then she said, "Some tight layers of latex too. If your heart could take it."

He reached for the dresser again, knowing that anyone, including the ballerinas and pandas and everyone else, could see that his legs were losing their resolve.

Then, she laughed.

"I'm just messing with you. I think maybe it's my coping mechanism."

A deep sigh escaped, then he said, "You're doing a hell of a job."

"Thanks."

He looked down when she took his hand, then up at her eyes.

"We didn't come here to see all this junk. Come on."

She led him away from Miley's bedroom to one of two closets near the entry.

"She kept her notes in here," she said, pointing to the door on the left, "like it's a little office. Check it out."

He opened the door and saw no coats or anything else hanging in what looked like another room, just much tinier. Aspin reached around and flipped a switch, turning on twin sconces set about waist-high to the left and right.

The golden light revealed a plush slab of carpet and more pillows leaning into the corners. A low, ornate table still possessed a pure white coffee mug.

With evidence that red lips had been swapping kisses for coffee.

A new-looking notebook leaned against the back wall, and a small box next to it held pens and pencils and erasers.

"Go ahead," she said. "See what you can see."

"Okay, thanks."

He stopped himself as he was about to enter Miley's office.

"So, this is all yours now?"

"Yeah, this is all my stuff. Don't worry, I won't throw out all that sentimental stuff."

"I hope not. So, uh, what happened with Miley? After that accident?"

"You disappeared."

Socrates stared, again fumbling around with his lips before he clamped them.

"I, uh, I couldn't help anyway, and I—"

"Relax, it's fine. They found my number on her phone and called me. I went down and ID'd the body and got her arrangements going."

He tipped his head, looking into her, or Miley's, blue eyes.

"You probably have an ID, too, then, right?"

She scoffed with a smile and said, "Sure, detective. Want to see it?"

He'd turned toward her, and she stood close, facing him.

"Well, I don't need to or anything. I was just—"

She lifted her short black leather jacket with both hands and said, "It's in one of those back pockets. Not sure which."

He looked down at the tight black denim matching every curve of her hips, then back up at her eyes. There was a grin there too.

"You, uh, if you want to show me, you can—"

"It's right there, Mr. Socrates. If you guess wrong, you'll have to check the other side."

She managed to control her laughing, but she did send him a big smile.

And he noticed that her eyes still looked at him without humor.

"Oh, hey. You could check both at the same time. Way down deep in those pockets."

He looked down again and said, "That would, I mean, it—"

"Wonder what that little card says? Now's your chance."

"I, uh, yeah. But I think—"

"Oh, you know what? Maybe I grabbed Miley's ID by mistake. Maybe that's what you'll find. What then, huh? Sounds like a philosophical dilemma."

His eyes were already threatening to pop out when his phone rang loudly in his pocket, and she stopped fighting to keep her laughter to herself.

He kept staring at her hips, then her eyes, and she said, "Well? Answer that goddamn thing."

She bottled up her amusement when he held up the phone and said, "Lynnie, hi."

* * *

Socrates kept his phone to his ear and grinned at seeing Aspin turn herself around, offering him the back pockets of her tight black jeans.

"You're what? Now?"

She snapped her hips a couple of times each way, then let her jacket drop as she fluffed back her hair.

"No, that's fine. Yeah, now's a good time to look over all that."

Aspin spun around and lowered then raised both hands, inviting him to look her over, as she mouthed the words, "Look over this."

Socrates's eyes flared open before he closed them and put his free hand over them.

She backed away, a hand over her mouth to help stifle her laughter.

"Oh, the birds? Yeah, Lynnie, I just fed them. I'm heading home."

He peeked through his fingers and saw that Aspin had retreated far enough to lower herself quietly onto Miley's couch. He frowned and shook his head roughly when she picked up a ballerina and got a grip on the winder.

He mouthed the word, "No!"

She pouted and put it back down.

"Well, Lynnie, they're always hungry. What's that? Oh, that ring. Yeah, it's with me, like I said. I'll explain when I see you."

He listened for a few seconds, watching Aspin cross her legs, then fuss with the shoe before kicking it lazily, her eyes on him.

"Okay. Yeah, I'll see you soon. Bye."

He tapped it and put it away.

"A girlfriend?"

"Lynnie? No. My daughter."

"Oh," she said as she stood and began the few steps needed to get in front of him again.

"What ring?"

He squinted at her for a second before reaching in for it to show her.

"Oh, wow, an engagement ring. Miley would have said yes."

"What? No, it wasn't for her!"

"Huh? How could that be? You didn't even know me yet."

He watched her big smile and said, "You, you don't really—"

"Messing with you. You can tell me all about that special someone next time we get together."

"Uh, next time?"

"Yeah, Mr. Socrates."

She had her hands on her hips, not offering a hint of a smile.

"You and me. We're going to retrace everywhere you went with Miley."

"Uh, why?"

"Answers. I need to understand what led to what you saw happen to her on that street."

"I told you: she wanted to—"

"Humor me, alright? Really, it's the least you can do."

He looked into blue eyes that could have been Miley's and said, "Okay. Sure."

With Miley's notebook under his arm, he pulled in the apartment door and said, "Text me sometime. We'll set something up."

"Wait," she said. "One more thing."

She took his arm and led him back inside the apartment, toward the other closet. After tipping her head at the door, grinning, she opened it, and Socrates looked inside.

There weren't a lot of skirts hanging in there, but they were all short. He saw blouses and t-shirts and tank tops, too, all of them solid, bright colors. And on the floor, several pairs of shoes with spiky heels were lined up and ready to step out.

And on the left side, separated from the common stuff, was a black skirt and a crisp white blouse, keeping watch over a pair of high black heels below.

He couldn't break his gaze of that special outfit when he heard Aspin say, "Yeah, that would be my choice too."

He turned to her and said, "Huh?"

"For Miley to wear. I mean, if she were here."

He winced at the blue eyes that were clearly enjoying seeing a wave of anguish about to swamp him.

She tipped her head and said, "You must know that that would all fit me too."

"Well, it, uh . . ."

"Every little curve."

"Uh . . ."

"Better run along, Mr. Philosopher. Who knows what might happen if you don't?"

He softly snorted out a breath and hurried back to the open doorway.

"Uh, okay, text me sometime, alright?"

Before answering, Aspin sat on the couch, gave a ballerina a crank, then set it down to play.

Then, she locked her blue eyes on his.

"I will."

Socrates tipped his hat, while holding his breath, then stepped into the hallway and closed the door behind him.

Then, he leaned his back into the door and listened to one of Miley's sweet melodies until it reached its end.

Chapter 10 – I Needed His Name

He looked up at all of the twisted strands hanging in a neat, orderly procession all around the perimeter of the fabric awning that shielded the entryway to his apartment building.

It had seemed that heavy water drops had collected on them for an eternity, but the rains had ceased, and sunshine had warmed the concrete sidewalks while he walked back home from Miley's apartment.

And from the company who, he had to be honest, could somehow have been Miley.

But what if he had fished out one or even two photo identification cards? What could he have concluded from that?

"God, I'm losing my mind. I wouldn't know what to believe no matter what I'd found in those pockets."

He snorted out a deep breath and opened the heavy door, which seemed lighter than when so much wind had battered it.

The lobby lights above, staggered all around the voluminous room and waiting only for lively music to begin a swaying dance, lit the room with more vigor than any natural sun.

And the walls and furniture and decor everywhere screamed out for him to compliment their colorful displays.

But he looked only at the burgundy couch, hoping to see Wendy.

And her cat.

But the couch was empty.

Still staring, he heard light steps coming down the stairs and a young voice saying, "Hi, Mr. Lewis!"

He'd started smiling before locking his eyes on her. He waved and watched her holding a black cat against her white hooded sweatshirt as she bounded down, not paying any attention to all of the fiendish purple circles looking up at her, probably trying to trip her.

"Hi, Wendy. And Rae Cat too."

They got to the couch at the same time, and she sat with the cat by her side.

"Taking a break from school, Wendy?"

"Yeah. Break time. Good!"

She petted the cat, then she and Socrates both looked toward the stairway at the sound of heavier footfalls.

Wendy's mother was making a descent, and Socrates tugged at his coat as inconspicuously as he could, making sure that none of those blazing suns above them would light up the polished metal of a flask that felt light, reminding him that it needed a generous refill.

And gum. Can't ever run out of gum.

Or mints.

"Hi, Mom."

"Hello, Wendy's mother."

She laughed as she walked toward them and said, "I should have properly introduced myself by now. I'm Rosa."

"Ah, thank you. Lovely name."

"Why, thanks. Socrates is quite a name, too, Mr. Lewis."

"Oh, that. That's not my real name."

"Yes, I know."

She took a seat beside Rae.

"Interesting choice, though. Got a good story to go along with that?"

"Other than the book about him I keep upstairs?"

"Well," said Rosa, "your story should probably include why you bought that particular book, don't you think?"

Wendy hit Rosa's leg with the back of her hand and said, "Mom!"

Rosa kept looking at Socrates and said, "She tells me I'm nosy."

Before Socrates could respond, he found himself laughing at Wendy's giant smile and nodding head.

Rae Cat didn't smile or nod. She only wanted Socrates to see that her eyes were green.

"We could just call that a reasonable curiosity."

"Yeah, I like that. So, what's the deal with the ancient guy?"

"Have you ever read anything about him?"

"No, I sure haven't," said Rosa, "but maybe we should work that into the curriculum. What do you think, Precious?"

Wendy scrunched up her face and shook her head, convincing Socrates to laugh again.

"No need," he said. "I'll tell you everything you or anyone else needs to know about him. His big thing was that he didn't know anything."

Rosa and Wendy stared. Just like the cat.

"He thought of that realization as being about the wisest thing any of us could do. So, I was going through a time when I felt kind of lost, like I just didn't know anything that I needed to know. I came across his philosophy, and I just felt like I needed his name."

"Makes sense. Glad to hear you got through that."

She waited, nodding her head slightly, looking up at him.

"Uh, I . . ."

"You're still there, kind of lost, huh?"

"Yeah, Wendy's—I mean, Rosa. I think it's kind of like quicksand."

"We learned about that," said Wendy. "It's scary."

"Yes, Wendy, it surely is. Sometimes, not knowing things can be a little scary, too, so make sure you study hard."

Rosa leaned toward Wendy and said, "I think Mr. Lewis is wiser than even the real Socrates from way back when."

Wendy turned to her and said, "And he feeds the birds."

Smiling up at him again, Rosa said, "Yes, he does. That's very nice. So, modern-day Socrates, what quicksand of not-knowing is pestering you these days?"

He looked past Rosa and Wendy and Rae on the couch and somehow, his eyes found, in a painting across the room, a swath of color quite close to the eyes of Aspin and Miley.

"Uh, I . . ."

He heard Miley's ballerina twinkling through a door.

He saw Aspin shake her hips, daring him to dig both hands deep into her back pockets.

A quick shake of his head brought him back.

"Oh, uh, mostly . . . what to write about."

"Write a story about feeding birds!"

"Thanks, Wendy. That's always good advice. Maybe I will."

"I can't imagine how you come up with things, Socrates. I guess that's your job, though."

"Well, it's supposed to be. Tell that to the blank sheet that's been lodged in my typewriter for—"

"Typewriter? No, not really?"

The lobby door whooshed, but no one looked.

"When I get an idea—if I get an idea—I'll first have to squeegee off all the dust so the ink letters can stick."

Rosa and Wendy both laughed, and Wendy kept it going as Rosa was saying, "Oh, Socrates, that—"

"Dad?"

All heads, even Rae's, turned toward Lynnie standing halfway between the door and the couch.

*   *   *

"Lynnie, hi."

He coughed to calm himself as he walked quickly toward her.

"Thanks for coming. These are my neighbors: Wendy, her mom, Rosa, and their cat, Rae Cat."

She waved, and two out of three smiled and waved back.

"Nice to meet you. Nice lobby," she said while looking around. "Sure is bright."

"Yeah, even when a lot of other things are gloomy. It's always sunny in here. Don't start thinking that my apartment is anywhere as nice."

"Oh, Socrates," said Rosa. "I'm sure it's quite nice."

Lynnie paused to glance at Rosa, then looked back at her father.

"So, about that research."

"Right, we do have to discuss that stuff. We'd better get started. You probably don't have much time."

"Never do. Let's get going."

She looked toward the couch and said, "It was nice meeting all of you. Even you, little kitty."

Rae Cat only stared at her, but the other two expressed a matching sentiment.

Socrates turned enough to elevate an arm for his daughter, but she only looked at it for a second, then bumped her shoulder into him.

"Good to see you, Dad. Cool that we're working together on something."

"You too, Lynnie. Yeah, I agree. Very cool."

They walked side by side toward the stairs.

And he felt something like a stab to his heart at just then realizing that he hadn't thought through all of that nearly enough.

Because dastardly purple circles were about to laugh loudly enough at his blatant failings that even Lynnie would hear.

He gave her feet a quick glance.

"Good."

"Huh?"

Socrates drew in a deep breath, grabbed Lynnie's hand, and towed his daughter behind him as she laughed hysterically and ran along with him.

Chapter 11 – Very Much Like a Hooker

"Oh my God!" she said between deep laughs.

Socrates slammed the door behind them and leaned over, choking in heavy breaths. He looked up enough to see Lynnie still laughing, shaking her head, and also out of breath.

"What the hell was that?"

He rushed out the words, "Just a second," then tipped his head forward and kept breathing.

She pulled her hand free and easily stood upright, even though he could still hear her breaths.

"Nice place."

"I appreciate your dishonesty. Thanks."

He stood as tall as he could, forced out a deep breath, and hoped that that would cap it off and end it.

It didn't.

"No, really. Not bad. But seriously, what the hell was with running up here like that?"

"Exercise? I really should make an effort."

"And you said 'good' at my shoes because—"

"Because you can run in those. Yeah."

"Well, I never would have known. Nice neighbors down there."

"Oh, uh, yeah. Mostly Wendy, the girl. I haven't seen her mother—"

"Rosa?"

"Yeah, that's it. I haven't seen her too often."

She watched him closely and said, "She seems kind of cool. She's pretty."

He kept his countenance unreadable, but said, "Well, so's your mother. There are lots of—"

"Mom really is pretty. Yeah. Glad you know that."

"Well, of course, Lynnie. So, we should probably—"

"Mom gave you a compliment the other day."

He began walking her toward the kitchen.

"Oh, really? What about?"

"Oh, nothing. Something about how you look in that hat, I think."

He fought to blink at a normal rate as he saw that very hat on Miley.

"It's a good hat. I wear it all the time."

They were both looking through to his kitchen, and he glanced at her briefly to confirm what he'd suspected: that she was staring at the blank sheet wound into his old-fashioned typewriter.

He held his breath and waited, but she held back her comments about that.

They'd be coming along soon enough, he knew.

"You should. Mom gave it to you."

"Yeah. Hey, you want something to drink?"

He watched her eyes veer away from the typewriter to the whiskey bottle just to its right, which reminded him of the flask hidden away in an inside coat pocket.

He carefully slipped off the coat and folded it over his chair.

"You know, what the hell. Yeah, okay. It's like a celebration."

"Fantastic. Have a seat."

* * *

He'd checked the glass from the cupboard by holding it up to the light, then buffing it quietly with a sleeve after verifying that Lynnie was looking through his notes.

Satisfied, he'd poured some for each, they'd clinked the glasses, and he fought to not swill down half of his glass.

"I'm not making much sense out of your notes. Sorry."

"I did kind of scribble them too fast while I was talking to Mara about it."

"Mara. The editor, right?"

"Yeah, that's her. She's rough, but I guess she's good at what she does."

She tipped her head toward the papers lying flat on the table and said, "That's for her philosophy magazine?"

"Uh, could be, I suppose. I'm not sure where my manuscript will end up. I mean, if we actually do this."

"What do you mean about it ending up somewhere?"

"Oh, the last thing I wrote up, I thought she'd publish. But she didn't want anything to do with it. So, she passed it off on someone else to try to make a book out of it."

"That's kind of weird."

"Well, yeah, but it's a weird story. Anyway, we should look—"

"First, the ring. You said you had it hanging up."

"I did say that I'd explain that, didn't I?"

"Yes, you did."

She took another sip, her eyes on him the entire time, and he sensed an opportunity to get some for himself too.

He blew out a deep breath, making her shake her head and chuckle softly, and said, "Alright, but this isn't easy."

She waited, without any particular expression and with her hand still around her glass. After seeing the level in hers, he gave his a quick glance and confirmed that his restraint hadn't gotten him too far ahead of her.

"Okay. It's about something that I don't think I've ever told anyone. It's only recently that I think I figured out what's been going on."

She nodded, holding his gaze.

"I always leaned to the left."

"Like, politically? That's not so—"

"No, uh, like physically."

"You'd fall over."

"I never did. Well, once, but that was an unusual situation because—"

"What does that have to do with hanging a ring somewhere?"

"I had that engagement ring tied to a shoestring, and that was hanging in front of my bedroom mirror."

"Oh, you'd use that? To check yourself?"

"See? It's not that weird, then, right? Because you get that I—"

"No, Dad. Sorry, but it's weird. You'd stand in front of it and see that you were leaning?"

"Yeah, all the time. I'd try to figure out ways to fix it. The best I could figure was that the wind had something to do with it."

He laughed softly at her shaking her head.

"I never noticed."

"I, uh, well, I moved out before you were big enough to notice something like that. It's easy to miss when you're just little."

"I think I would have noticed."

"Did you?"

She grinned and said, "No. So, what the hell? Why were you leaning like that?"

"All this time, I never knew. But Lynnie, it was from when I got lost once when I was little. I was walking on this low wall in a park, and I fell off."

"To the left?"

"No, that's the thing. I fell to the right."

"Oh, so all this time, you were making sure that you didn't fall like that again?"

"Weird, huh?"

"Yeah. It really is. You're done with that, though?"

"I think so. It's been better for a while. So good that I took down that ring."

"To carry it around with you."

"Uh, yeah. In a way."

He pinched it from inside his shirt and let it drop.

She looked first at the ring, then into his eyes.

"You're wearing that everywhere you go?"

He saw a smile that he was sure she was fighting.

"Yeah. Lately."

She nodded and let the smile out.

"Good. You might need it. Best to keep it ready."

He smiled back at her, then pointed at her.

"I know what you're thinking."

"Me? I'm just wondering why you call yourself Socrates. Do you even remember your real—"

Someone rapped quickly on his door.

* * *

His heart rate climbed as he hurried to answer the knocking, visualizing a pair of tight black jeans, the back end, pointed at him and his daughter.

Maybe even shaking around a bit.

It couldn't wait more than a second, he knew, so he did turn the knob and open the door, only to see Rosa standing there.

Her calm smile helped to settle his heart.

But he knew better than to look down.

Too much was always going on down there on that goddamn carpet.

"Rosa?"

"Hi, Socrates. Sorry to bother you two."

"No bother."

Then, remembering the hazardous floor covering, he said, "Please, come in."

"Well, okay."

He didn't mean to bump the door into her as he swung it shut, but she just wasn't moving quickly enough.

"What's on your mind?"

Before answering, Rosa leaned to look in on Lynnie and waved to her. Socrates watched his daughter wave back, just once, quickly, not taking any time to add a smile.

He didn't notice that he'd been holding his breath until Rosa turned back to him and gave him a bright smile.

"I'm reluctant to ever impose on a valued neighbor, but—"

"But?" said Lynnie, and both Socrates and Rosa turned to look at her.

She shrugged and held her eyebrows up until they looked at each other again.

"But Socrates, I was wondering if you could watch Rae for a short while?"

"The cat?" said Lynnie.

"Yes," said Rosa, looking at her then back at Socrates.

"Just for a few minutes. Something came up, and I need to drop Wendy over at her father's for a while."

From the kitchen, Lynnie said, "Can't be easy to keep two homes."

Rosa only looked her way for a few seconds, then said, "Uh, he has his own place, if you must know."

"I don't have to know."

She turned back to Socrates and said, "We've been separated for a while. His schedule is—"

"Oh, not divorced."

Both looked in at Lynnie, who looked at each of them, then shrugged.

"That's correct."

"The cat, huh?" said Socrates. "She's not okay alone?"

"Oh, no, she is. It's just that I baked a bunch of cookies, and they're all laid out to cool. I probably should have timed things a little different."

They both turned to look at Lynnie, but she only shrugged and smiled.

"Well," said Socrates, "I suppose we—"

"We were talking about going out for lunch, weren't we, Dad?"

Looking at Lynnie, he said, "Uh . . ."

"Oh, well, I don't want to be a bother," said Rosa. "I just hate to put her in that cage, but if I have to, I can."

"Problem solved," said Lynnie and when they looked, they saw her tipping up her glass for a sip, the notes in her other hand as she looked them over.

"I guess I'll just get going, then."

"It was good to see you, Rosa. Good luck with the logistics."

"Thanks."

She let herself out, and Socrates avoided any sight of the red, orange, and yellow bits of plague at their feet until he could close the door after her.

He stayed against the door and laughed softly, shaking his head at Lynnie's smirk.

"Lynnie. That was—"

His phone rang and rattled on the table and before his daughter could pick it up, he scurried in and saw that Aspin had sent him a text message.

∗   ∗   ∗

He angled the phone so that Lynnie had no chance of seeing that Aspin had sent, "I'll be at your building in ten minutes."

He replied, "No, it's not a good time."

"Dad, tell Rosa you meant it when—"

"Oh, uh, no. That's not Rosa."

"Alright. It can't be Wendy or that cat of theirs. Mara?"

He laughed and said, "No, Mara's usually too nasty to type. She's happier just saying it. Sometimes screaming it."

"Alright, I give up. Yeah, I'm nosy. Who is it?"

He remembered the confusion he'd felt when Aspin had thrown down birdseed, then said that she never feeds the birds.

"It's just someone that feeds the birds the same place and about the same time as me."

"You guys have some kind of club or something?"

"Something like that."

He saw that Aspin still hadn't replied, so he typed, "Don't wear Miley's clothes."

He hit "send" and barely listened when Lynnie said, "Some kind of bird-feeding emergency came up?"

Accepting that Aspin wasn't about to confirm or deny that wardrobe choice, he looked up at his daughter.

"Uh, kind of. People and their birds, right?"

He waited for something more than the blank stare she gave him. She finally spoke.

"Those aren't anyone's—"

"Uh, can we postpone this research, just for a short while?"

"Sure, Dad. I didn't plan on staying long anyway."

*　*　*

He'd timed it perfectly, waiting until Lynnie had stepped through the doorway before claiming that he'd somehow forgotten his hat.

"Go on ahead, Lynnie. I'll be just a minute."

"Sure, Dad."

"Wendy and Rae Cat are probably down there already."

"I like that cat's name," she said over her shoulder.

Socrates closed the door, ran to the bedroom for the hat, then into the kitchen for the flask in his coat pocket, which he saw wasn't nearly full enough.

"No time for that now," he said as he slipped it back into its dedicated inside coat pocket.

He swung in his front door.

"God, that carpet's still there."

In the hallway, eyes closed and his back to the closed door, he took ten deep breaths, then held the eleventh.

He was halfway over the multi-colored minefield, nearing the stairway, when he remembered that he'd forgotten to lock the door.

But no one watching his mad sprint would have seen the slightest hesitation.

Until he stopped at the top of the stairs, spending a second acknowledging the malevolent circles, all pale purple, waiting for him to count, then calculate their areas, then add them all up and place each step just exactly—

"Don't fall, Mr. Lewis!"

He looked over at the young girl on the burgundy couch, a black cat on one side and a daughter of his on the other. And he knew that any attempt at speech would shriek out uncontrolled from the pressure he'd imposed on his lungs.

So, he let it all whistle out and drew in a fresh portion. Under less pressure.

"I always try not to, Wendy!"

"God," he said softly to himself, trying like hell to be his best possible ventriloquist, "just keep my eyes on that girl. Or that cat. Or that daughter that's jealous of Rosa."

He smiled in spite of his predicament, managed to keep looking and waving at the three pairs of eyes burning into him, and quickly shuffled to the bottom.

Confirming his safety by verifying that he was standing on the tile floor, he heard Lynnie say to Wendy, "He's got this exercise thing going on lately."

He heard Wendy giggle before he could look that way, and he saw that both girls were smiling.

But not the girl named Rae Cat.

He walked toward them more slowly than if he hadn't needed to catch his breath.

"Never too late to get started on that," said Lynnie.

"Yeah, I think so too. Wendy, you're going to see your dad, huh?"

She looked down at the cat that she was petting and shrugged.

"Uh-huh."

Socrates shared a look with Lynnie, which was interrupted by Rosa traveling down the stairs which had very nearly snared Socrates at every step.

And they both heard Wendy say to Rae, "Time to go."

Socrates glanced at his watch and saw that about ten minutes had passed since Aspin had texted him, so he made sure that no one was watching him and looked through the glass toward the sidewalk.

And his heart nearly stopped at seeing Aspin, midway between the building and the street, her back to them.

He quickly looked toward Rosa and said, "Sorry about not watching that Rae Cat."

"Oh, it's fine. She'll be okay for a few minutes. Come on up, Honey. Let's get that kitty set up."

"Aw, Mom. Just another minute, okay?"

Rosa walked toward the couch, saying, "Honey, no, we have to get going."

Wendy sighed, scooped up the lounging black cat, and walked toward the stairs.

Socrates shot a quick look out again and saw that Aspin hadn't moved.

And she looked very much like a hooker.

"Lynnie, maybe you should take those notes? For that project?"

"I could. Sure. Just unlock the—"

He laughed and said, "With all that exercising, I'm sure I left it unlocked. Just lock it up when you leave, alright?"

"Sure, Dad. You have to run?"

"You meant that to be funny, right?"

"Yeah."

She gave his arm a squeeze, then aimed for the stairs just as Wendy and the rest had begun the hike along the balcony railing.

And Socrates exercised again, getting himself out of that building just as quickly as he could.

Chapter 12 – She Isn't a Philosopher

His eyes on Aspin, who still faced the busy and noisy street, Socrates eased the door shut behind him. He looked her up and down, took one step toward her, then stopped himself. After another quick scan, he spun to the right and began a determined walk, weaving between passersby.

But the image of her wearing Miley's select outfit—the short black skirt, neat white blouse, and spiky black heels—began a haunting of him that he suspected might never release him.

"Hey, wait," he heard her say behind him.

He stopped and turned and saw her walking with a confident strut, convincing him that she was even more adept than Miley with that style of dress.

Watching her hips swaying easily, he winced at wondering where she might be hiding her identification.

Or Miley's.

Or both.

"Hi, Aspin. I'm, uh, kind of surprised that you couldn't wait."

She'd caught up with him and stood near, holding one hand up above her eyes to block the sunlight. A light black leather jacket was folded over her other arm.

"I got to see that Lynnie's a real person."

"Oh, yeah, she sure is."

"You had all kinds of company in there. Even a little—"

He got a solid grip on her arm and brought her along in a brisk walk.

"We should probably get out of here."

"Ooh, forceful. Don't want all those women folk to see you with a hooker?"

He stopped her, saw her grinning, and said, "You're not, I mean, you couldn't—"

"Makes you wonder, huh?"

He felt his lips doing their new thing, vibrating and quivering and saying nothing.

She looked ahead along the sidewalk and said, "Still, you ought to get started on some explaining."

When she resumed the walk, he hurried to catch up and walk beside her.

"What does that mean?"

"You can start by telling me why you were fleeing the scene back there."

"Fleeing? I was walking."

"You saw me. I know you did."

"Oh, yeah, but I—"

"You probably did some reminiscing, eyeballing what I'm wearing."

"That's, uh, that outfit that was—"

"You could have introduced me to everyone. Even that cat."

He stopped, she took another step then stopped, too, looking back at him with a smile.

"Alright. Fine. I never even told Miley this."

"Tell her now."

"You really should stop," he said.

She shrugged and said, "I could try."

"Way back when, I was engaged to Lynnie's mother."

"That ring? Oh, it really wasn't for Miley."

He shook his head but couldn't help smiling.

"I knew Miley for only a couple of hours."

She stopped nodding and held his gaze for a moment.

"Bet that was enough time."

He squinted but couldn't look away from her eyes.

"Like I was saying. It was for Valerie, but she . . . saw something she shouldn't have."

Aspin shook her head once and said, "No time for mysteries. Spill it."

"Fine. She caught me with a hooker and ended it."

She laughed at the sunny sky before shaking her head at him.

"Beautiful. And you're out running wild with Miley, and—"

"It wasn't like that."

"I bet you did some running. Wild? Hell, you saw her end up dead."

"Yeah, we ran some, and she . . . I didn't think—"

"How wild would it have gotten if you'd had more time, though?"

He groaned and nudged her to walk with him.

"I can see why you ran out on your daughter like that. Did she see the hooker waiting for you?"

"First, you're not a hooker. And even if she did see you, why would she think you were waiting for me?"

"Maybe I'll tell her."

"You're not funny."

"Not a hooker either. I might be Miley, though. You're not sure."

"Stop."

"Okay. Hey, take me to where you first met Miley."

"Alright. It's not far. It won't be the same, though."

"Yeah, I read her notes. It was all rainy and gloomy then."

"Yep."

"I should have brought her fur coat too."

She looked over just long enough to see him shaking his head as they walked toward the alley where he'd first met Miley.

"She told you most of the crosswinds. There's more about them in her notes. But there's something else. I don't think she wrote it down."

"Like what?"

"It's about light."

"What about it?"

"It's just something weird. She came up with some weird shit. How about that fiancé of yours?"

"What about her?"

"Well, Mr. Socrates, I bet she isn't a philosopher."

He didn't answer, and they kept walking side by side.

After a few steps, she took his hand.

"She's probably not a hooker either."

She looked over at him, but he kept his eyes on the sidewalk ahead. So, she snapped his hand up then down quickly and glared at him.

He looked and only stared at her for a few seconds, then she replaced the sour face with a modest smile.

"Certainly never dresses like one," she said.

He sighed and shook his head at her.

"Come on. That's funny."

He didn't answer, and it took a moment as he again watched the path ahead, but he eventually managed a smile.

"It's the other way," she said. "Out of your building, then left."

"Yeah. True. But we're not walking past there. Not right now."

"Because you're with a hooker? Lynnie would rat you out to Valerie?"

"Something like that. Yeah."

Chapter 13 – There. Feel Safer?

"Just ahead," he said.

They'd walked around the block, and he'd made no effort to cast away Aspin's warm hand.

"Miley wrote about a bird flying into the alley."

"Yeah, one did. A big black one. Hey, do those notes I took home have what she wrote about meeting me?"

"No way. I'm keeping that."

Socrates scoffed and said, "Lovely."

"I'm surprised you're still holding my hand."

He tried to get his hand free, but she resisted and ended up squeezing onto just two of his fingers before he yanked his hand away.

"I, uh, kind of forgot."

"Uh-huh. Hey, let's do this: you wait here, and I'll go in and stand in there like Miley did."

"Why?"

"Just to try to understand what she went through. Humor me?"

"Sure. Go ahead."

She rounded the corner and began her walk into the alley, which even with a clear sky above was flirting with all kinds of shadows.

Socrates leaned around and watched, finding the sight of her legs, bare beneath Miley's short skirt, almost hypnotic.

"God, I never did see Miley's legs in daylight. Huh."

Aspin took a few more steps until she was at about the midpoint, then leaned against the wall on the left. Socrates took his first step to go to her, then froze when she lifted her right leg and rested her heel against the bricks, leaving her knee jutting out in front of her.

"Jesus."

He resumed his walk and said, "I mean, God. Damn, either way."

Standing near her, he leaned to try to see her face better, but she kept it aimed at the opposite wall.

"What happened next?"

He laughed at remembering it.

"I bumped my shoulder into the wall to straighten myself up."

"Weird thing to have to do. Not this time, though?"

"No, I think that's done. Hey, you, uh, where did—"

"I found them on the ground."

He stared at the rusty scissors in her hand, and he sighed slowly at seeing that she didn't have the business end pointed at any part of herself.

"I, uh, but I was watching you, and—"

"Because you like Miley's short skirt?"

"Uh, actually, I—"

"Not the skirt. Miley's legs."

"Um . . ."

"Or Aspin's legs. Identical."

"Yeah."

"Take a closer look, if you want. See if you can find any difference."

"I, uh . . ."

"Later, then," she said.

He cleared his throat and said, "But really, you didn't pick anything up."

She flipped the scissors around, pointing them randomly, and turned her head toward him.

"Maybe I picked them up before. Not today."

"Oh, yeah. Because Miley wrote about that, right?"

"That would explain it, Mr. Socrates."

He took another step, leaned against the wall again, and she turned to face him. His eyes were drawn to her smile, Miley's smile, but a glint lower convinced him to look.

And he saw the points almost touching his trench coat, aimed for his abdomen.

"I'm not suicidal," she said, and he looked into her eyes.

"Uh, I don't want to die either."

He felt her pressing them against him slowly until his coat was pinned to him.

"Uh, maybe you should put the scissors down."

"Is that what you told Miley?"

"Word for word, I think."

"Do you really think Miley wanted to die, Mr. Socrates?"

"Uh, Aspin. This isn't funny."

"I'm not laughing. Are you?"

He shook his head slowly, avoiding any sudden moves, and said, "No laughing here. I didn't want Miley to die."

Socrates held his breath and watched Aspin's blue eyes look at each of his own repeatedly, and he let it seep out when her sharp glare softened and her lips relaxed into a smile.

"There's a difference."

"Uh, what do you mean?"

He looked down and focused on the sharp instrument until she pulled it back, then let her hand drop to her side. He noted that she hadn't dropped the scissors, then looked back at her eyes, which had shifted back to a colder stare.

"Between not wanting her to die and . . ."

She tipped her head and waited.

"Stopping her?" he said.

With her other hand, she pointed at his face and said, "Bingo."

"She . . . she said 'bingo' too. For something else, though."

"There's a reason why I know that."

She was again smiling, and he glanced down to see that she still hadn't thrown away Miley's possible suicide weapon.

"Because you're sisters?"

She stared for a long moment, then said, almost in a whisper, "Maybe."

Socrates squinted at the blue eyes staring back at him.

"She threw the scissors down. So, maybe . . ."

Aspin dropped them, and they clattered, but she'd never looked away from him.

"There. Feel safer?"

He watched her lips for longer than a moment but saw no hint of a smile.

"Um . . ."

He recoiled when she laughed toward the sliver of blue sky stretched between the building tops above them.

"There's no right answer to that one."

She shook her head, giving him a big smile, and took his hand, which again felt soft and warm.

"Come on. She said something about a bar that you two spent some quality time at."

"Yeah, you were there. You said so."

"I did say that, didn't I? Yes, I sure was there."

She turned and started walking, and he wasn't about to let go, so he followed along, taking a few ambitious steps to get to her side.

*　*　*

"How much farther?"

He stopped her and waited until she turned to him, and he didn't let go of her hand.

"Wait a second. Was that really you that tipped Miley off that she should leave the place?"

She nodded and said, "I do watch out for her. I did, I mean."

"But that doesn't ans—"

"Come on. I think I see it right up there."

He stayed behind long enough to glance down at her legs, which were stabbing the heels into the grimy asphalt much like Miley would have done.

Over her shoulder, she said, "So, what was her final verdict?"

"Miley's? About what?"

"God or Satan?"

"We never found out who that priest worked for."

"Me neither. That was one creepy son of a—"

"You've seen him?"

"It. Yeah."

"When? How?"

He stopped, tightened his grip on her hand, and forced her to a complete standstill too.

"That thing had been—"

"That's what Miley called him," he said. "A thing."

"Well? You thought that thing was human? Entirely human?"

"I don't know. No, I guess not."

"Like I was saying: that thing bugged her all the time. Yeah, I saw it but just once."

"So, who do you think he worked for?"

"I'm more curious what Miley thought. From her notes, I think she thought it was an angel."

"Why?"

"She wrote some other things about Jesus. She kind of leaned that way, like he was made up."

She saw him about to speak and hurried to say, "Not leaning like you. What else would she have said just now? Oh, yeah. You madman."

"Yeah. Yeah, I'm a madman. What else did she write?"

"She wrote that the whole idea of Jesus was kind of cruel."

"How?"

"Suppose you'd never heard of him? She wrote that a hell of a lot of people lived and died long before Jesus supposedly came along. What about them? And even now, she said, how about someone on some island somewhere, never hearing about any of that. Or how about someone whose mind isn't right, and they can't even fucking understand the story? Their asses just get busy burning in Hell?"

He looked away from her calm eyes to scan along each side of the alley. There were boarded-up doors, others rusted and seldom opened. Full trash cans, some empty. And dirt and trash everywhere.

"Uh, that would suck."

"Yeah. And even if you heard the story, with all the fucking lies out there, what if you just don't know what to believe?"

"Uh, I don't know. It's hard to know anything for sure."

She tugged on his hand, getting him to walk with her while saying, "You wouldn't know anything about him. You'd have to go straight to Hell."

"You're right. That's kind of cruel."

"You mean that Miley was right. You don't mean me, do you?"

"Um. I think—"

He heard her scoff, then she said, "You're probably going to Hell anyway."

*　*　*

They stood at the top of the three concrete steps that led down to the bar's entrance. Despite adequate daylight, the bare bulb above was lit and appeared bright against the dark bricks. All except for dust that had been crusting itself into a crown for a long time.

"That's it?" she said.

"You have to ask?"

She turned to him and said, "If I was Miley, I'd know that was it. If I'm Aspin and said I was there, I'd know that's the place."

He stared. She stared back.

"Kind of leaves you not knowing much, huh?"

Before he could answer, she laughed and said, "You picked that name. That's on you."

"Socrates?"

She shrugged, then smiled.

He let his breath trickle out with a dry, raspy sound.

"You're fun to mess with."

"Thanks."

"So," she said, "what did you talk about in there?"

"She told me that she asked for an idea, and she got it."

"She said that she asked for it, huh?"

"Yeah. Why?"

"Nothing. That's good that she wanted an idea."

"Sure. And I told her a story about when I was a kid."

"What about?"

"I got lost, and I never realized how much that affected me."

"Like how?"

"It caused all that leaning. Oh, and monsters too."

"What monsters?"

"When I was just little, and lost, I thought they'd eat me. That night with Miley, I heard them everywhere. I even saw them a few times."

"They didn't eat you?"

"No."

"Weird shit. Okay. Then, what?"

"Then, we had to leave because—"

"Because someone told her that—"

"Hey, are you doing this on purpose? Messing with me?"

"Yeah, Mr. Socrates. It's fun. Where did you go after that?"

"You really want to retrace our travels?"

"Sure. It's like déjà-vu for you, isn't it?"

When he looked down at her legs, she angled one out and up, then twisted Miley's black high heel from side to side before stepping it back down. He held the sight a while longer, then looked up.

"All around town with a hooker. Twice. Like a dream come true for a guy like you."

"Uh . . . not the same hooker, though."

She smiled but didn't respond.

"Right?"
"I like that you don't know," she said. "It's amusing."
He stared, his lips moving, making an effort.
"Next stop on our tour is?"

Chapter 14 – Jesus. Your Answers...

Over the sound of vehicles in the busy street, Aspin said, "That one?" and pointed ahead to a fabric awning over a building's entrance.

"Yeah, that's it, but hold up a second."

They stopped and stood side by side, facing the street. He pointed at the curb.

"It was raining, and there was all this trash floating along there, washing down into a sewer."

"Yeah?"

"She asked me where it all went."

"I bet you didn't know."

"Jesus," he said and started a slow walk toward the canopy. "That's what I told her."

He heard her heels coming up behind him, and she said, "Back with Jesus, huh?"

"Why not? I never know which—"

His phone rang in his coat pocket, so he took it out and tapped it.

"Lynnie. Hi."

Aspin watched him as he turned to look at the street.

"Yeah, I haven't gone back home yet."

He felt her bumping into him, so he looked down and saw that she was holding out a small amount of birdseed. He gave her a smile, she bounced her eyebrows twice, then he held out a hand for her to pour it.

"The birds, still. Yeah."

He threw the seed down and gave her another smile.

"I'll call you. We'll get going on that soon, alright?"
A few seconds later, he said, "Okay, bye, Lynnie."
He tapped it and put it away.
"You think of everything?"
Aspin said, "That's not the most important question, is it?"
"Uh, what is?"
"Why the world saw Miley as a piece of trash too."
"I, uh, I don't think the—"
"Did you?"
"What? No!"
"Alright, let's get under there."

*　*　*

"We stood right about here."
"I was on this side?"
He stared at her until she laughed.
"You know what I mean. Miley was here?"
She took a place to his right, close enough to bump into him.
"Yeah, and she, uh . . ."
"She what?"
"She held onto my arm."
She slipped her left hand around his arm near his elbow.
"Like this?"
He laughed and said, "Both hands."
"Good," she said, using her other hand, too, "you're getting into it. We have some serious reliving going on here."
She smiled over at him but saw that he was frowning, looking toward the road.
"Oh. Bad choice of words."
"It's fine, Aspin. If that is your name."
"It's a good name."
She laughed at him only shaking his head at her comment.

"So, Mr. Philosopher from Ancient Times, what all happened next?"

"She talked about that crappy drug experience."

"Did she remember any details about that?"

"Well, she heard that idea, and she—"

"Who told her?"

"She didn't know. She thought it was either God or—"

"Who else was there? Was anyone else there with her? Did she remember?"

He looked over and was met with a pair of intense blue eyes, and he could see that her breathing had become more intense as well.

"Jesus, what's the big deal? She was high. She didn't remember much."

Her sigh was obvious as she looked out again toward the street.

"Mostly, though," he said, "she went on about not liking being a hooker. She didn't say it exactly, but I think she felt like she was kind of damned for living that way."

Aspin nodded, then said, "Well, you never heard of Jesus, so you're going to Hell too. We'll all be there."

He turned to her and found that her face was quite close. And it was Miley's face.

"All three of us?"

"Could you handle two of me?"

"Jesus," he said and laughed as he looked out at the traffic. "Your answers . . ."

"You didn't want me to just shut up, remember?"

"I remember. It's just . . . you don't really—"

"I bet you tried to comfort her about being a hooker. You did, didn't you?"

"How the hell do you know me so well? Unless you're really—"

"A psychic?"

He sighed and said, "Yeah. That's what I was about to say. Well, you're right. I told her that she looked good and that counted for a lot."

He waited, looking ahead, and didn't hear anything from her, so he looked.

She'd been waiting for him to look, and she said, "So, I look good? That counts for something?"

"Yeah, Aspin. Damn. Yeah, you look good."

"You don't mind walking with me some more, then?"

"No. Not at all. Where to?"

"You tell me."

"Miley told me here that she had to show me that priest guy and what that's all about."

"A suicide attempt?"

"Uh, yeah."

"Let's do it."

He stared at her and didn't see a trace of a smile.

"You don't . . . you don't mean—"

"I mean, let's go. Unless you're thinking of something else?"

It took a while, gazing at her up close, but he eventually saw a smile.

Chapter 15 – You Want to Pretend

"That one," she said as she pointed into the alley, "right there?"

"Yeah, that's it. It's easy to see today. Not like two nights ago."

"Miley saw it, though?"

"I watched her looking into the dark, and she knew it was there, but I don't know how. I didn't see anything."

She took his hand and started walking, saying, "This should be fun."

"It wasn't."

Still looking ahead, she said, "I bet. I'll make it fun this time."

"Uh, 'this time?'"

She kept walking and said, "Yep."

*　*　*

As they walked through the alley, side by side, he took several glances down at her hand, surprised that she hadn't taken his.

He remembered that Miley would have.

"You said she climbed up there?"

"She even tried to jump for the ladder, but that didn't work."

"Heels and a skirt. Same ones I'm wearing. Weird, huh?"

He held her steady gaze and said, "Uh, yeah."

A moment passed, then she said, "We're kind of waiting."

"Yep. I'll get it."

Socrates jumped and got both hands on the lowest rung, and he hung there as it creaked lower and lower. After it had hit the asphalt, he stomped on it a couple of times before Aspin bumped him to one side.

With both hands on the ladder, she said, "Two stories up? That's where she went?"

"Yeah, right there," he said, pointing at the metal grating serving as a landing where it was bolted to the bricks.

She gave it a look, then smiled at Socrates and waited.

"What?"

"You don't hear it?"

He looked each way along the alley, seeing traffic crossing at each end and hearing nothing else.

"Traffic, you mean?"

She laughed at his confusion and said, "Maybe I need to wind it up again."

It took him a second, then he snapped his eyes up to the windows high above them.

Looking at her again, he said, "No. You're not serious. That's Miley's apartment?"

She nodded and said, "Hard to keep track with all the streets and alleys, isn't it?"

While he was again looking up at Miley's windows, she started her climb, carefully placing her spiky heels to keep her secured on each rung.

"You holding it?"

"Yeah, Aspin."

She took a few more steps.

"Don't let it go—it seems kind of shaky."

He tried to shake it, and it barely moved.

"Feels okay to me."

She took another step, and her bare thighs were even with his staring eyes.

"Maybe I'll rest for a second."

He looked quickly each way down the alley and saw that no one was watching. So, he turned back to her legs and looked down only when she kicked a heel up behind her, held it, then let it down slowly.

"I bet Miley stopped right about here too."

"No," he said, "she, uh, she didn't."

"Oh, that's right. She was in a hurry to kill herself."

"No, I think she mostly wanted just to show me that priest guy. And when she got up there, that priest did—"

His phone rang out in his pocket, and he looked up to see her smiling down at him. Then, she gave him a shrug.

But she didn't take another step.

He got it out and gave it a tap, then held it to his ear.

"Mara, hello."

He nodded a few times, listening.

"Yes, I know. I'm not capable of too much research. That's why—"

Aspin plucked his hat from his head, so he looked up. She smiled down at him as she reached up to put it on.

"—I asked my daughter to help. I mean, if we decide to follow through on that."

She held it close to him again and when he reached for it, she snapped it up too high.

"Okay. Uh, I'll try to decide by—"

Aspin passed the hat to her left hand, and she held it down by her side, next to her left leg. He reached for it with his left hand, causing him to have to lean closer, and she moved it out farther.

"—the end of—"

He listened while making another grab, leaning closer again and causing Aspin to giggle.

"Oh, um, I'm just kind of distracted. Yeah, the park is, uh, kind of crowded today."

He made a quick grab, very nearly planting his face against Aspin's thigh, and was successful in snagging his hat.

While he was saying to Mara, "Okay, sure. Yeah, I'll write that other—" Aspin took the hat from him again.

"—story even sooner. Okay, I better go. Bye."

He put the phone away and looked up, unable to keep from laughing at seeing Aspin wearing his hat again.

"It starts with just a little lie like that, Mr. Socrates. Obviously, you were born with at least a touch of evil, weren't you?"

"I, uh, what?"

Wearing his hat, she continued the climb up the ladder, and he silently watched every part of her legs passing by, close enough to kiss.

*   *   *

"Shame on you," she said as she neared the landing.

"Why?"

"Watching me. You are, aren't you?"

He snorted out a single laugh.

"Well, if I was born evil, I mean, yeah. Why not? Hey, what did you mean by that?"

She ignored him and cupped her hands against one of Miley's windows to look in.

"Oh my God. How could she be in there?"

"Miley?" he shouted. "Miley's in there?"

He started to hurry up the ladder until he heard her laughing.

"Messing with you. Just my reflection."

"Not funny."

He stepped back onto the pavement.

"Sorry. But it's a little funny."

She turned away from the glass and took the few steps needed to stand against the railing.

"Like this?" she said as she climbed up onto the lowest cross piece.

"Hey, don't. That's not funny either."

She pointed down at him and said, "You'd think so if that priest showed up."

"Wait a second. You really have seen that priest?"

"Dark glasses? Doesn't say much?"

"That's him. When did—"

"What a loser. A total freak."

"That's what Miley called him—a freak."

She stretched her arms forward and apart, then looked each way.

"Hey, who's going to save me?"

"I will," Socrates said as he began climbing.

"Stop!"

He stopped, standing on the second and third rungs.

She backed herself off of the railing and stood where she could look down on him.

"Is that what you said to Miley?"

"Uh, I didn't want her to—"

"Sure, she said to stop, but did you try to climb up and stop her anyway?"

He felt his lips moving silently again as he looked up at a face that had been smiling only seconds earlier.

"I, uh—"

"Goddammit, Socrates, did you try to stop her?"

He clenched his jaw, stopping his lips, but he couldn't stop staring up into her blue eyes that could have been Miley's.

"No. You didn't."

He took a step closer to the alley floor, eyes still locked on hers.

She stood with her hands on her hips, glaring down at him.

"She, um . . ."

Aspin spun to her right and approached the nearest window of Miley's apartment.

"I'm going in. We can talk about it in there."

She tried one window, then the other and got it to slide up. From below, he watched her throw one leg over the sill, lean her body in, then pull in her other leg. A spiky black heel was the last thing he saw.

He stared up at an open window in an alley that muffled and dampened traffic sounds trying to drift in from both directions.

*   *   *

He stepped down his other shoe, but he didn't let go with his tight grip on the rusted metal. His eyes were fixed on the open window, and he leaned each way, trying to look inside Miley's apartment.

But there was only the one-time invitation and a silent window leading to an apartment, a fantasy home, where only Aspin waited for him.

"God, what am I doing?" he said as he began traveling up to the landing.

He rested his shoes on the rough metal grating as he looked each way along the alley.

No one around. No one watching.

He looked up at a sky that had invited a few puffy clouds to scrape along the building tops, and no one looked down from up there either.

Maybe just God, he thought.

Leaning to look in, he saw Miley's living room area just as he'd seen it before.

But there was no sign of Aspin.

He thought for a second, recalling the layout, then took a few steps to his left and looked into Miley's bedroom.

He raised both hands up to press his palms against the glass, and he squeezed his nose into the pane as he froze in place.

Aspin was seated on the edge of Miley's bed, facing him and from not more than a few steps away. She kept her heels together and close to the bed, displaying her knees and thighs, and she looked him in the eye as she slowly removed a fake fur coat.

"God, that's . . . that's . . ."

She let it drop behind her, looked to one side, and brought up a red heart sticker. Her small smile sent a shiver all through him, then she let it fade as she placed the sticker over her lips.

Calm blue eyes gazed at him as she carefully smoothed it, touching it softly with her fingertips.

"Oh, God. That sticker . . . that keeps you from . . ."

She shrugged once, just once, and reached for the top button of her blouse, which she popped open.

Socrates nearly crumbled from the next shiver.

Aspin worked open the next button down, her head tipped, her blue eyes burning into his. A warm kiss hidden by a heart.

And Socrates spun himself away from the sight and rushed to the railing, getting a death grip on it with both hands. Heavy breaths brought in the damp alley air and shot it back out as he stared at the cool bricks across from him.

At the sound of someone passing through the open window, then closing it, he shivered and looked up at the sky.

And a voice, which could have been Miley's, said from behind him, "If I shut the hell up, who am I?"

He looked down at the trash containers by the other side.

"You're . . . Miley."

"Hey, Socrates, you want to pretend, I think. Not look below the surface?"

"Um . . ."

She took a place beside him and also held the top rail, their arms pressed together.

"I felt like she was back for a while," Aspin said as they both gazed at the weathered brick wall. "I miss her."

He sighed and squeezed the railing.

"Do you?"

"Yeah," he said. "She—"

"Left this world too soon. Yeah."

His sigh mixed with the words, "Too soon."

"I guess I got lucky finding that sticker in Miley's place, huh?"
Facing her, barely able to speak, he said, "God, unless . . ."
She bounced her eyebrows once. Just once.
He wiped at one eye and felt his hat placed back onto his head.
"What's next?"
He turned back toward her and was met with staring blue eyes.
After zipping around the brim of his hat once, he said, "To the
bridge."

Chapter 16 – Disguising Himself in Light

"It was seriously raining the whole time you and Miley wandered around the city?"

"Mostly, yeah. Sometimes, it was really light, though."

They walked in generous sunshine along sidewalks teeming with folks traveling in both directions. Beside them, all sorts of vehicles formed steady streams, each rumbling out its own tune.

"There," he said, pointing ahead. "We sat there for a while."

She felt him take his hand.

"Then, so will we."

He felt her hand warm and smooth in his and he knew that if he closed his eyes, and if he'd ask Aspin to just not speak for a while, it would be Miley's hand.

With or without a delicate heart sticker on her lips.

"Oh, it can't be," he said as they approached the bench.

He picked up a square of cardboard that someone had left there.

"What?"

"We used this when we sat here. Well, no, not this one. But Miley held up a piece like this to block the rain."

She snatched it from his hands and bumped him with her hip, causing him to sit.

"She did that too."

"With the hip. It's kind of a girl thing."

He nodded at her as he drew in and held a deep breath before letting it dribble out.

"Weird," she said, then sat beside him. "Like this?"

She held it above them both, blocking only sunshine.

"Yeah. Then, I apologized to her."

"You probably should have. Tell me what about."

He removed his hat and held it out over her lap.

"About not offering it to her sooner. But now, that's not really an issue."

She laughed and said, "Because I already took it from you once."

She dropped the cardboard, then placed the hat on her head with both hands.

"But you gave it back."

It took a second for her to turn and look at him.

"Only so you could offer it," she said.

She smiled, then said, "Even if you're kind of evil."

"Alright, I don't get it. What the hell are you talking about?"

"Don't feel bad. I think we all are. We couldn't avoid it."

"You think so?"

She shook her head and said, "Miley thought so."

"It's in her notes? I'll read about that later?"

"No, she never wrote it out."

"So, tell me."

"Nothing's free. You tell me something first."

He looked down at her legs, which weren't wet like Miley's had been. Instead, the sunshine was giving them an appealing sheen.

"Alright. I told her why I like hookers. You want to know?"

She turned to him again and said, "You're saying I'm a hooker?"

He squinted for a second, then said, "Did I say I like you?"

She held the hat as she looked up at the sky and laughed for a few seconds.

"Oh, that's rich. Yeah, Mr. Socrates. In so many ways. Shall I list them for you?"

He coughed and said, "Uh, no. That's fine. So, I told Miley I liked hookers because it doesn't matter whether they care about me or not. I said that I'd never even ask one."

She nodded, looking forward, and said, "Makes sense. There's someone in your life who has never said it, and you're still waiting."

He stared at her as she looked only straight ahead, and he studied every line of her face, looking for any slight difference from what he'd seen of Miley's.

There wasn't any. They were truly identical.

"Jesus."

"You're waiting for Jesus to tell you that he cares?"

"What? No. I was just—"

"Using his name. I get it. Well, thanks for sharing that. All I can tell you is don't wait forever. It might never happen."

He stared at her lips to watch her finish the last word.

Then, he stared a little longer.

"Uh, you're probably right."

"Where's that bridge?"

"About ten blocks ahead, that way," he said and pointed.

"Not in these heels," she said and stuck one leg out, which he studied closely.

"Oh, uh, we took a cab."

"Alright, then so will we."

"That got kind of weird. Maybe we should—"

"Alright, back to Miley," she said and turned to him. "She was always talking about Satan. She said he went by all kinds of names, like—"

"The Old Serpent?"

She stared for a second, then said, "Huh. That's a weird name. She said that?"

"Yeah. Said she read it somewhere."

"Doesn't matter. So, she learned about him disguising himself in light, trying to look like a good guy."

"Which he's not."

"Maybe to some people. Anyway, she learned that that light of his, the devil's fake light, it—oh, perfect. Here comes a cab."

She stood and took two steps toward the curb, then turned enough to spin Socrates's fedora back to him. He caught it while standing up to follow her.

* * *

When Aspin reached out over the street, hailing the approaching cab, Socrates tried not to look down at her legs, which were becoming more uncovered every time she waved her arm around.

He didn't succeed, and he studied her form until she turned to him, something he'd made himself watch for.

"Perfect timing," she said.

"Yeah. How about that."

"I can't believe you got in a car with a suicidal woman."

"She was persuasive."

Aspin clanked open the car's back door and said, "Am I?"

Socrates only shook his head and smiled, then she got in, shimmied over, and smiled up at him.

He got in and slammed the door shut.

"To the bridge up ahead," she said to the driver.

"Sure," he said and put the car in gear, then pulled out into traffic.

He felt her warm and pressed up against him, her body and her leg, and he leaned to speak quietly to her.

"She had a wild idea when we took that ride."

"Yeah? Tell me."

"She wanted the driver to speed up, and she was going to grab the wheel and try to roll the car over."

"Why didn't she?"

He pointed at the back of the driver's head.

"Guess who it was."

She scoffed, then laughed softly.

"Unbelievable," she said. "Not human, though. That's for sure."

"Didn't seem like it. Hey, you don't think . . ."

He watched her focus on the driver, squinting at him, then she turned back to him.

"No, I think that freak is gone for good."

"That thing about Satan and light and all that. That's not another crosswind, is it?"

"No. Neither one of them would—"

"God or Satan?"

"Yeah, neither one would care who told the world about it. It's people that wouldn't want to hear it."

"Well, you have me curious."

She turned to him, their faces close, and he watched her look over his features, taking her time before she spoke.

"You're curious who I am?"

He scoffed and looked ahead to stare out the windshield just as she tried to kiss him. She settled for his cheek.

"I do love messing with you."

* * *

"This is close enough," she said, loudly enough for the driver to hear.

They heard the brakes beneath them begin to squeal and watched the driver steer them toward the curb. Up ahead, the bridge waited.

"Looks like we're here. Bridge time."

"This should be something," he said.

"Uh-huh. With me, something else."

Then, to the driver, she said, "Hey, what's your name?"

He turned his head enough to see Socrates, and said, "Maxwell."

"You're not a priest, are you?"

"No, lady. Uh-uh. What's your name, since we're being so social?"

"Well," she said, turning to look at Socrates, "that's the real question, isn't it?"

Socrates laughed and held his face with both hands.

Maxwell turned back around, but Miley tapped him on his shoulder, holding out a few bills.

"Keep it. Thanks."

"Anytime."

She leaned into Socrates, who dropped his hands and opened the door. On the sidewalk, he saw that Aspin had only extended a hand toward him, so he took it, helping her out to stand beside him.

The cab's engine revved modestly, its turn signal flashed, and Maxwell pulled it carefully out into traffic. They stood side by side and watched it become just another car roof in a river of them.

"So, tell me about the bridge. Oh, wait. I can guess. A hooker leaping off a bridge."

Chapter 17 – Something to Dream About

"That was funny," she said as they walked toward the bridge. "That Maxwell guy."

"How so?"

"When he asked me my name. I bet your ears were straining to hear what I'd tell him."

"Yeah, they were. But you don't really answer questions much."

"Kind of a mystery. That's me. But I get that that kind of bugs you. So, go ahead and ask something. Here's your chance."

He stopped just before stepping onto the bridge's sidewalk, and she stopped with him.

"Alright. What's your name?"

She shook her head a few times, grinning.

"It's Aspin."

Socrates let out a deep sigh.

"Honestly?"

"Yeah," she said. "It's just . . ."

"Just what?"

"Maybe Miley's name wasn't really Miley."

"Oh, Jesus," he said, laughing. "Good one."

"Can't ask her anymore."

His laugh dwindled to nothing.

"No. Because she's—"

"Gone. Yeah. No one saved her."

"That priest guy was supposed—"

"I'll take some of that whiskey."

"Sure."

He handed it to her, and she shook it around, scoffing at how little was left, then finished it. She capped the flask and was about to throw it over the railing near the walkway, but he grabbed her arm.

"Hey, don't. I always refill that."

"Good thing you stopped me, then."

She handed it back to him, and he tucked it away.

"Miley threatened to throw it away. Same place too."

"Huh. Someone that called herself Miley?"

"You're making me crazy."

"I'll show you crazy if you don't get that thing filled up pronto."

He turned to look at the city behind them and said, "There's a beverage shop a block back and a block over."

"Got them all mapped out, Mr. Philosopher?"

He grinned and said, "Just the ones I need."

* * *

Small bells high on the shop's door jangled when Socrates jerked it open and held it, allowing Aspin to enter first. He smiled at the sight of her strutting, and doing it well, for whoever inside might be watching her grand entrance.

Before turning right, toward the whiskey shelves, he watched her slow to a stop, still facing the clerk, who smiled and waved to her.

"Hey, Miley. How's it going?"

"It's good. We just need some whiskey."

"Kind of a late day for you, huh?"

She turned to smile at Socrates, who was staring and shaking his head.

Before looking away, she said, "Hey, I'm running a business here. Profit comes first."

The clerk snorted and said, "Yeah, forget the schedule."

Then, she looked again at the clerk, who shrugged and began helping a customer who'd just walked up to him.

Socrates zeroed in on his preferred brand, then saw that it was out of stock, so he grabbed the label next to the empty space. When he turned, he found that Aspin had walked up behind him and was waiting.

"Miley, huh?"

"What can I say, Socrates?" she said. "Twins."

He tipped his head, studying her unwavering gaze.

"You went everywhere with her?"

She scoffed, then smiled.

"Think that through a second."

It didn't take him a second.

"No, you didn't. These people would know there were two of you."

"That would sure prove it."

"Yep."

"So," she said, grinning, "I must have sometimes . . ."

"Went to the liquor store for her?"

"Sure. Keep going."

"Went to her apartment. I saw that with that neighbor."

"Right. What else?"

He looked away from her blue eyes to watch her lips cast off her smile a bit at a time.

Looking into her eyes again, he said, "You sometimes took her place? At her . . . job?"

She only nodded and said, "Something for you to wonder about, huh? Oh, maybe even something to dream about."

"Don't I have enough scrambling my brain already?"

"Your name is Socrates. You don't know anything, remember? Let's just keep it all scrambled up."

* * *

Socrates passed the bottle to her as they neared the bridge again. She tipped it back for a second, then capped it and gave it back to him.

"I'll throw it over the edge when we've had enough," she said.

"It'd be evil to throw out good whiskey."

"Maybe it's evil just to drink it."

They walked in silence a few more steps, almost at the beginning of the bridge.

"You really should tell me about that other Satan thing."

"I should. But of the three of us, who's the most evil?"

"Me, you, and Miley?"

He watched her nod as she laughed.

"Probably you," he said, also laughing.

"You might be right. Probably twice as much as you. Okay, there's this—"

She took a step to the right and looked over the railing and the ground falling away.

"What?"

"Thought I saw someone."

"The priest?"

"Not likely. Hey, maybe when I'm about to jump. Come on."

She turned and began a focused walk but stopped after two steps and looked back at him.

"Well?"

"She . . . I think Miley held my—"

"Yeah, she was like that. Here."

She took his hand, and they began a slow run toward the middle of the bridge.

Chapter 18 – Where You Saw Her Die

With the feel of Aspin's warm hand squeezing his, leading him on across the bridge, Socrates tried to look around and remember the exact location where he'd stopped with Miley.

"Here. I think it was here."

She stopped when he stopped, and she let his hand free.

"The highest spot. Right."

"She wanted it to be as dramatic as possible."

"Was it?"

"Oh my God. Yeah."

He put both of his hands up on the rail and looked over it at the silent train tracks far below. The clear skies and sunlight were generous with the terrain, and he scoffed at it appearing not the least bit ominous.

But he did scan everywhere that he could and sighed loudly at not seeing anyone dressed like a priest. He let the last of his breath seep out before he turned toward Aspin, who had stood with him, close enough that their arms were brushing against each other.

And he found that she'd been staring at him. Waiting.

"What?"

"She stood here? At the highest point for the most spectacular high dive?"

"Uh, yeah. She said she—"

"But you tried to lead her back down there,"—she tipped her head toward the beginning of the bridge—"to stop her from jumping, right?"

"Well, no. She—"

Her eyes had become a shade hotter. The stare more of a stabbing.

"Did you do anything to stop her, Socrates? Or were you just going to watch her sail down to crunch herself up down there?"

"No, Aspin, no. I tried to grab her arm when she was up on the rail, but she—"

"You let her climb up on the rail? That's what you're telling me?"

"I guess. Yeah. She wanted to prove to me that that priest would—"

"And what if that thing hadn't helped her? What then, Mr. Philosopher?"

He stared at her, his cheeks ballooned up, under pressure.

"She was handing my hat back to me, and that's when I tried to—"

"Give me your hat."

"Uh, sure."

He reached it out and held it in front of her, but she didn't take it. She only glared at him.

"Um, okay."

He carefully set it on her head, watching her eyes the entire time. He'd never seen them blink.

With the hat securely in place, Aspin looked out over the train valley and toward the skyline. Its brightness and cheer didn't find any way to put a smile on her face.

She started to climb the rail.

"Hey, uh, maybe—"

"Time to fly."

"No. No way."

Instead of grabbing at her arm, he reached around her and locked her in a hug, then he spun to get her off of the railing. He'd just set her down, heard her heels striking the pavement, and held her long enough to be sure that she had her balance.

When he was just about to release her, he felt first the brim of his hat touch his shoulder, then he heard it drop to the asphalt.

Then, her head rested on his shoulder.

He didn't release her.

Almost whispering, she said in his ear, "That's what you should have done."

He felt his lips fumbling again, and all he could do was nod.

He hoped that she'd felt that. And when she began to twist herself away from him, he let her go. She took a few steps backwards, her eyes boring into him.

"You didn't really try."

"Um, maybe I would have, but that creepy priest pushed me out of the way. He saved her."

Aspin turned to look toward the end of the bridge and the busy crossing street beyond it. The street where Socrates had seen a speeding bus annihilate Miley while he and the priest stood and watched.

Eyes on him again, she said, "That's where you say she died?"

"Yeah. That street."

"You watched her die?"

"She wouldn't let me help her. And that priest guy didn't even try."

"Show me."

"Huh?"

She turned and started walking toward that street.

"Uh, no thanks. I don't think I'll ever want to see—"

She stopped abruptly and spun back toward him.

"Show me where you saw her die."

"No, Aspin. Please. I don't want to—"

Squinting her eyes into narrow slits, focused on his, she said, "It's all your fault."

"No, Aspin! How could it be my fault? She—"

"It's your fault because you're evil."

She jabbed a finger toward him.

"You were born evil."

"I was what?"

"All of us were. Most of us try to at least stop people from killing themselves. Not you."

She lowered her hand, then shook her head.

"No. Not you, Socrates."

He only gazed at her with his heart pounding and his breaths quickening.

"Come on. Get your evil ass moving."

"Aspin, no! I—"

She turned and began a solid march, and he stared at her legs, long and bare, ending in Miley's heels, as she left him there on the bridge.

But she stopped after ten steps.

She turned. Her face twisted into a scowl.

"Get over here! Now!"

Socrates started to back away, shaking his head.

"Don't you dare leave, dammit. We're going to that street."

"No," he said softly to himself, still backing away.

"Where you saw Miley die. You fucking watched it happen!"

He stared at her twisted, angry face for only another second, then he turned and began running the other way.

Behind him, he heard Aspin screaming that he was evil, that it was his fault, and that he might as well have killed Miley by his own hand.

*   *   *

Aspin's screaming faded, then became unintelligible, but Socrates never slowed his sprinting.

Not until he heard distinct scraping sounds rising up from over the railing just ahead.

"Oh, no. God, not again," he said as he slowed himself then stopped.

"Those animals have been gone since I made peace with them at that mailbox."

He took another step.

The scraping grew louder.

"No, they can't be back. God, please don't let them be back."

He blew out a deep breath, shook all over, then approached the location. His shaking hands held the rail for several long seconds.

Then, he inhaled, held the pressure, and jutted his head out to look down at whatever foul beast would be waiting there, probably ready to snag him with a bloody claw, pulling hungrily, the fabric ripping but not enough to free him, then he'd fall with the beast while it gouged and shredded and—

It was only a sign, rusted loose and flinching nervously in the breezes.

"Huh. Not a monster."

He laughed at the sight of it.

"Not going to eat me."

At the sound of Aspin's shrill yelling, he turned and saw that she was stomping toward him. She hadn't yet crossed the bridge's midpoint, but she would. Soon.

Socrates fled as if actual beasts or monsters were in ravenous pursuit.

* * *

He held his coat, and the bottle and flask in inside pockets, tight against his chest as he ran through the city. His path veered between every obstacle—disinterested pedestrians, aromatic food carts, staring newspaper vendors—as he raced home, sometimes near the curb and other times scraping along the cool brick walls.

Claws. There were claws reaching for his back.

He turned his head quickly to look and saw no monsters.

"Maybe I'm just too fast for them. God."

He sprinted a few more steps then, sure that he'd be eviscerated in a second, he arched his back to evade the swiping talons.

"Leave me alone!" he yelled, and he didn't care to see if anyone thought he was a madman.

He ran. He wove around everyone and everything.

"That's what Miley called me: a madman. Jesus."

Why aren't they running from the monsters too? he wondered.

Then, he remembered that they were his monsters.

111

Only his.

If they were still there.

He looked ahead and saw the entrance to his building.

"Wendy," he said, puffing it out with his rapid breaths. "And Rae Cat."

He zipped past the mailbox where he'd had his last encounter with that odd priest. And those monsters of his too.

In the lively sunlight, the volume beneath the fabric canopy shielding the doorway appeared as a large, semi-dark block, something, he thought briefly, that might trap him like a tar pit, leaving him to suffocate, then fossilize as eternity sped past, then reveal his tragic end when archaeologists picked around and dug out the remains of his body and the bottle and the—

A death grip on the door's handle allowed him to yank it open, and he almost dove inside, suspecting that he'd lose his spine and all kinds of squishy things connected to it if he were to linger out there another split second.

He pulled the door shut behind him, and his eyes pleaded with the burgundy couch.

And his prayers, to either Jesus or God or both, were answered.

Wendy was already smiling at him.

And Rae Cat was staring. Like every other time.

Chapter 19 – You Rested Enough, Mr. Lewis!

Wendy's wave and calling out erupted at the same time.

"Hi, Mr. Lewis! You were exercising again!"

Socrates laughed and began the short walk to the couch. He wanted to look up at the tiny suns watching him from above, each on its own chain trapeze, but the sight of the little girl's eyes were warmer than any artificial sun that he could imagine.

"Hi, Wendy. I'm so glad to see you."

She grimaced quietly, with her eyebrows way up high, and tipped her head toward the black cat, who was lying to her left, pressed up against her.

And staring.

"Oh, and you, too, Rae Cat. Hello."

He waited, his smile growing as green eyes stared silently back at him.

"Well, I think she said hello. In her own way."

"She doesn't always talk," Wendy said while rubbing the cat's back. "But she kind of talks."

Socrates was standing near the couch, looking down on the two, but only the cat was returning his gaze. Until Wendy looked up too.

"Wendy, have I ever told you that I'm very glad that you're my friend?"

Her eyes got big, and she said, "Um, kind of. Like Rae."

He laughed, shook his head a few times, and said, "Without words. Yeah, I believe I have. I'm glad you know that."

She nodded.

"And I hope you'll always be my friend."

She tipped her head and studied him for a few quiet moments.

He stared down at the child, holding his breath.

"Will you always feed the birds, Mr. Lewis?"

"The birds? Feed them?"

She nodded, still petting Rae.

"Why, yes. Yeah, I don't have any reason to ever stop."

"Okay."

"Okay?"

She giggled and said, "Okay, I'll always be your friend."

Socrates held a watery gaze of his friend on the burgundy couch, then wiped once under each eye, making it look like only a few lazy scratches.

"Good. And I'll always be yours. How about that cat of yours?"

Wendy glanced at the cat, then up at Socrates with a shrug which she froze in place for a long few seconds.

Her serious face broke into a grin, and she said, "I don't ever know for sure with her, Mr. Lewis."

"No, I don't suppose so. It's sad when people are like that too?"

She leaned forward to look into the cat's eyes, then faced Socrates again.

"Maybe mostly if they have blue eyes?"

He'd already started rubbing his eyes, covering them, when he said, "Yes, that, uh . . . yeah, blue eyes. I'd better go, Wendy."

He turned, his eyes still shielded from examination by an eight-year-old girl or a cat of undetermined age. He stopped his walk to the stairs when Wendy spoke, but he didn't turn to her.

"Mr. Lewis?"

"Yes?" he said, facing away and toward the stairway.

"You already exercised."

"Oh, uh, yeah. I just did some running."

She didn't speak again, and he waited until his curiosity had grown far too large. One last wipe at his eyes gave him some hope that they'd recovered, and he turned to look at her.

Her face was solemn, and she was pointing toward the far wall of the building's gargantuan lobby. He looked, and he saw it.

Facing her again, and seeing that she'd adopted a happy smile, he said, "The elevator, Wendy?"

"Yes, Mr. Lewis. You need to rest."

"Oh, you might be right. The stairs are good for exercising."

She nodded and said, "And the elevator is good for resting."

"You're very wise, Wendy. Maybe I should allow myself that luxury."

After watching her smile and say, "Rae Cat likes to be spoiled," he tipped his head at the sight of them on the couch.

"Keep spoiling her, Wendy."

He glanced quickly at the stairs but began a swift walk toward the elevator.

*   *   *

Looking down only long enough to avoid folding himself over a couch or a chair, or splintering a shin against a low coffee table, or elbowing over a lamp, Socrates walked as straight of a path toward the elevator as he could manage.

Halfway there, the memories came back.

All of the problems posed by a simple contrivance called an elevator.

A voice inside screamed for him to go tangle with the horrific purple circles on the stairs instead.

At least he could see all of them. He had a slim chance of succeeding in counting them, calculating their areas . . . doing all of that.

But he didn't scream and run for the stairs, partly because he knew that he was being watched.

Wendy.

And that Rae Cat.

That black cat never, ever stopped watching.

He stood in front of the clean, polished metal door, his fingertip almost touching the little round button with an up arrow etched into it.

And he hesitated, feeling two pairs of eyes, maybe more that he hadn't noticed, burrowing into him, first through the coat, then the shirt beneath it, then his skin, which he knew would sizzle and smoke and—

He tapped the button.

And started counting in his head.

He knew that his lips were following along, but there was no time to deal with that.

Will it be ten seconds? he thought. Fifteen, maybe? I can't see where the cab is—I can't possibly know.

He watched the door, waiting for it to slide open so that he could get in, hit the button for the second floor, then . . . what?

It had taken months to purge the memory of the bizarre, chaotic lines of the carpet square lining that damn elevator's floor. Dizzying lines, impossible to organize by color or length. All different widths, some even tapered—a reference sheet of formulas would be needed to calculate areas.

He remembered only that almost instantaneous insanity awaited beneath him if he were fool enough to step in there.

But if he did entomb himself in that infernal box, how long would it take to get to the second floor? Five seconds? Ten? More? Less?

Then, will there be a pause before the door opens? How long of a pause?

And what if it didn't open, fiendishly waiting to sense the pained halting of his heartbeat before allowing anyone to see his body, cumpled and twitching on the colors and shapes that had murdered him?

Was that elevator cab actually a sly coffin, waiting for his foolhardy compliance?

And if he could somehow survive the journey, when the door to the second floor finally opened, after tormenting him mercilessly, what would he see?

A hallway carpet carrying on its back laughing red shapes, sneering orange shapes, and, the worst of them all, the yellow globs that he knew would be cursing him, his very existence, the fact that he even dared to set foot on them, as if he could ever count them quickly enough to—

The door lurched before moving, then began to slide to one side.

And Socrates didn't slide to one side.

He ran for his life and soul and heard the giggling without having to look in Wendy's direction.

"You rested enough, Mr. Lewis!"

He got to the bottom of the stairs, his heart pounding and demanding the kind of rest that the girl on the couch had assumed that he'd already had.

Those purple circles. So many of them.

And each step runner was different.

There was no possible way to memorize some kind of travel scheme.

No time. Never enough time. Not with girls and cats watching.

Both studying him. Looking for any abnormalities in his steps.

No, it was impossible. He knew that he should have—

He laughed once, loud enough to fill the lobby, and reached inside his coat. Not for the bottle. For the notes. The notes about Mara's project.

He held them low, in a place where his downturned eyes could believably be reading them. But his eyes were scanning left to right, counting and adding and selecting the best possible location for his first step.

Which he took.

Wendy giggled, but he kept up the appearance of reading the notes.

While he counted, tabulated, enlisted the supposed usefulness of math, a subject which had always scorned him and exiled him in shame.

But he tried, and he made a sound choice for his second step.

Wendy had suspended her giggling.

But she was still staring his way, he knew. She and that cat of hers.

Using the pretense of studying notes, Socrates took his time and completed his voyage to the top, all with the accompaniment of a heavily beating heart.

He scoffed softly and said to himself, "God, I can't believe I'm just now thinking of this silly charade."

He'd just started to stare hopelessly at all of the red, orange, and yellow shapes on which he stood and across which he'd need to navigate, when a giggle from below in the lobby gave him an excuse to look that way.

Wendy was waving and smiling, so Socrates held up the note sheets and said, "Very important. Lots to read."

He smiled at the girl giving him a thumbs-up sign with each hand.

*   *   *

Having already explained the papers that he was about to hold right up against his face, touching his nose, almost, and blocking out the hallway's carpet, he held them up and stretched them wide with both hands.

He listened for giggling, heard none, and began careful steps toward his door.

"Huh. I can't see anything. Maybe I should always—"

"Mr. Lewis? Socrates?"

He recognized the voice. Wendy's mother. Rosa.

He peeked over the edge, still employing the full length of the sheets to block the vexing patterns below.

"Oh, hello, Rosa. How are you?"

She stopped as she was walking toward him and placed both hands on her hips.

"Must be something pretty important. Oh, is that something you're writing?"

"Oh, uh, no. It's some notes that I need to study for an upcoming project."

He never lowered the papers any farther, and he knew that Rosa must have been perplexed at seeing just his eyes, the rest of his face blocked.

She squinted at the sight and shook her head a few times.

"Well, that's quite an accomplishment."

"I, uh, what? What is?"

She pointed at his notes and said, "Reading sideways like that. I don't believe I've ever seen anything like that."

He held them out farther and studied them. Then, he tipped his eyes up to meet her curious stare.

"Oh, well, there's some scribbling sideways here, that's all."

He turned the papers to a proper portrait orientation and again peered at her over the top edge.

But his peripheral vision showed strong suggestions of the myriad traps that lay waiting beneath the soles of his worn shoes.

"Oh, yeah, that makes sense. Okay, I'm just going to check on them."

"A kid and a cat."

"Yes. Them."

She began to pass him, aiming for the stairway, and Socrates kept the papers up, his eyes turning to watch her moving past him.

"It was good to see you, Rosa. Take care."

She laughed softly and said, "I'm not sure anyone has ever seen me in quite that particular way. Have a good afternoon, Socrates."

He pulled the papers closer and shuffled until he could grab his doorknob. He gave it a quick twist, a quicker push, then lunged inside.

The papers scattered and drifted toward the floor as he leaned his back into the door, slamming it, and he waited with closed eyes for his pulse to stop taking everything so seriously.

Chapter 20 – Both…Of Them

"Oh, sweet Jesus," he said as he slumped to the floor, dragging his coat on the door until he came to a rest, his legs splayed.

He looked around at his apartment, which had welcomed inside some of the brilliant light being served up from a sky devoid of a single cloud. Glancing beside him, he saw his notes about Mara's odd assignment lying nearby, so he grabbed them up, placed the sheets in order, then laid the pile on his lap.

He gave his eyes a good rub, then the memories of all that he'd just survived on various carpets caused a loud laugh to get blurted out.

Until he remembered what had happened not long before that.

"Aspin. God, what the hell?"

Shaking his head didn't really help, but he tried it anyway before rising up and looking toward the kitchen. He knew what he'd see, but it still felt kind of like a punch. Or a kick.

The typewriter, with its constant tag-along, that blank sheet of paper, was busy doing its usual leisurely dust collection.

"Right. Like I'm about to write anything wondrous after all that."

While walking into the kitchen, he slipped out the whiskey bottle from one side and the empty flask from the other and, without having planned it, he held the bottle close, inhaling and hoping some scent would remind him of Aspin.

Or Miley.

"Shit, the scent would probably be the same too."

He clinked it down next to his usual brand, his faithful partner for so long. Next, he hid the flask behind canned goods in a cabinet, then took a step back.

"Huh."

The new whiskey, making its first guest appearance, was thumbing its nose at the old standby, bragging about its higher level inside.

"That just isn't right."

He sat at his typewriter but never gave it the slightest glance. Instead, he fumbled around for his glass, his eyes never leaving the bottle from which Aspin had swilled a fair share.

"God, it's like she kissed it."

He left the glass to uncap the bottle, then he poured and set the bottle back in its new place. It was still higher, so he poured more.

"Jesus. This isn't easy."

He saw that he'd poured too much, and the new guy's level was now too low.

"Easy to fix."

He uncapped his usual and poured some, then thumped it back down.

"Uh-oh."

He'd poured too much.

"Dammit, I'm fixing this."

He lifted the glass and made its contents all go away. Quickly. Then, he picked up the bottle that he hoped still carried Aspin's kiss.

Holding it close, he laughed dryly and said, "It's like I'm kissing her? Isn't it about the same as kissing Miley? Am I kissing both of them?"

He laughed and gave himself a heavy pour of it.

In his other hand, the uncapped regular variety waited for some attention, which it got. And then some.

"Huh. I like kissing both of—"

He winced and slowly tipped his eyes up, and he froze like that, an open whiskey bottle in each hand.

"Damn. Both . . . of them."

* * *

Each bottle got set on its own side of the typewriter, got held for a moment to avoid any tipping and disastrous spilling, and Socrates reached for the top of his head with both hands.

"My hat!"

He looked all over the cluttered tabletop, then on the single additional chair. The chair rocked and tried to evade his attack when he jerked aside his trench coat to be sure.

Then, he jumped up, ran into his bedroom, and rummaged around in the chaos that he'd intentionally left there. Because he had to. He had to learn to leave things to their maddening ways.

The hat wasn't there, so he leaned forward and looked into his reflected eyes.

"Oh, shit."

He stood up straight and scoffed at seeing that he was, indeed, standing up straight.

"Aspin. Aspin has my hat, that thief."

He reached inside his shirt, pulled out the engagement ring, still knotted onto a white shoestring, and gave it a long look.

"That blue-eyed thief."

He looked back into the mirror and said, "No. I offered the hat to her."

His eyes sunk back down to the shiny ring in his hand, which he'd kept since Lynnie had been just a little girl, younger even than Wendy.

Still gazing at it and the sparkles of sunlight it was shooting around the room, he said, "I offered her . . . the hat."

*　*　*

"What the hell am I even thinking?" he said as left the bedroom for the comfort of the kitchen table and everything that it offered.

"God, she just went insane and up in flames. And that face of hers. Well, it was Miley's face. What she was doing with Miley's face was just—"

The phone in his pocket chimed, so he took it out and looked at it while sitting at his trusty, patient writing contraption.

He tapped the phone and saw a text from Lynnie saying, "Hi dad. I'm in the lobby. Wendy and her cat are fun. I'm coming up when we're done."

"Oh, Jesus," he said out loud before tapping to reply to her.

"Hi Lynnie. They sure are fun. Okay see you soon."

He sent the text then set down the phone, where he launched that hand into a vigorous display of nail tapping.

"God, the hat. She might ask."

He jumped up and hurried to the small closet next to the entrance door and snapped it open. His heart calmed slightly at the sight.

"Nice. Organized. Not maddening."

He took a step back to get a better view of it.

"Lynnie can tell her mom I'm trying. But dammit, I deserve one little part of my life that is happily enjoying an orderly peace."

He looked at his watch, then reached into the closet, tipping things, lifting things, and sliding things to the side. But everything always got planted back in its proper place.

There was no backup hat.

He'd known that before beginning the frantic search.

"Dammit."

The phone chimed and rattled on the kitchen table, so he slammed the closet door and ran to get it.

"Oh, Jesus. What now?"

He opened the text from Aspin which read, "It's your fucking fault that Miley's gone. Get your drunk ass back here where you watched her die."

"Oh, God, what the fuck?"

He stared at the phone while fumbling around for his glass. With his hand wrapped around it, he set the phone down and raised the glass.

"Dammit."

It was empty, so he slammed it down and poured from both bottles.

"Yeah, both of you. Dammit, hurry up!"

* * *

Socrates swirled his whiskey around for a moment, staring at it spinning inside the glass. He shivered, drank some of it, then picked up his phone and gave it a tap.

He texted back to Aspin, "I didn't kill Miley! She had free will! Even the priest said so! It's his fault!"

He stared at the phone long after he was sure that Aspin must have read it. And surely, she'll write back, he thought. Right away.

She didn't.

So, he took another swig.

And he stared at the damn thing while pacing from room to room.

When it demanded his attention, he almost spilled what little was left in the glass.

He tapped it and read, "You want to know why you're evil Socrates? Why we're all born evil? Get your know-nothing ass here right fucking now."

"Jesus, what does she want from me?"

He started typing a reply but stopped at the sound of his door swinging in, then set it on the dresser and hurried out to see.

"Hey, Dad. I'm here."

Chapter 21 – Kiss a Goddamn Bus

Socrates looked up from the blank sheet wound and waiting in his typewriter on the kitchen table.

"You sure look ready to write something, Dad."

Lynnie sat in the only other chair in the small kitchen. She'd pushed aside some things on the table, including two plastic containers of birdseed and two whiskey bottles which didn't match.

"I sometimes think so, Lynnie. It's just that distractions kind of get in the way and make it a chore when it shouldn't be."

"Yeah, I get that."

He watched her grab one bottle, the old, trustworthy brand, and bump it closer to the newcomer. Then, she leaned forward, studying the contents.

"You want to toast to your new project?"

"Sure, Dad. Why the hell not?"

She kept adjusting the bottles, looking at them closely.

"Something wrong there, Lynnie?"

"It's just . . . they're . . ."

"Different levels. I know. It's always something like that that just—"

She turned to him quickly, ignoring the whiskey.

"Huh? Who cares? No, I was just wondering how they could be different shades, that's all."

"Still, both whiskey, though. They're probably just—"

"Different recipes. Yep. Hey, why are there two?"

"Two bottles?"

"Two different brands. I thought you'd have a favorite and never change it up."

"Oh, um, the liquor shop ran out of that one,"—he pointed at the old brand—"so I grabbed that one as a backup. You know, just in case."

She nodded, and a smile started to appear.

"And you couldn't help dipping into the backup supply. Right, Dad."

"Lynnie, I wanted to test it, make sure that it—"

"I'm teasing you. I don't care."

She got up and walked to the line of cabinets, opened one, and retrieved a glass, which she blew on and wiped on her jeans on the way back to the table.

"I could have got that."

"You need to rest," she said.

"I do?"

"According to Wendy. She says you've been running a lot lately."

He laughed and said, "Oh, Wendy. Yeah, I'm still trying to get in some exercise."

At the same time, she poured from both bottles, each into its own glass. After capping them, she laughed and scraped the glasses around in circles so many times that neither one of them could have remembered which was which.

"I can still tell," he said.

"Yep. By the color."

They each held up a glass and clinked them together.

"To our project," she said. "Whatever the hell it is."

They tipped back the glasses, and Socrates watched to see if she'd finish hers. She didn't, so neither did he.

His glass back on the table, but still in his hand, he said, "Well, I have some notes from Mara that we can—"

"Hey, where's your hat?"

"Uh, my hat?"

"Yeah. I mean, if you're going to be like some investigator type, wandering around looking for clues and stuff, shouldn't you be wearing that?"

"Oh, I don't know. That would—"

"Aw, come on. Wear the hat."

"I, uh, think maybe it's—"

They both turned to look toward the bedroom doorway when his phoned chimed in there.

"It's with your phone?"

"Well, I'll go see."

He hesitated, watching her hand, which was near her glass but not moving. After a quick look at his own glass, he left it alone, got up, and hurried into his bedroom.

*   *   *

He stood facing his mirror and picked up his phone. A quick tap displayed the message from Aspin: "Where. The fuck. Are you."

"Holy Jesus," he said softly, then leaned to look into the kitchen, where Lynnie was looking the other way and sipping her drink.

He started typing a response but was interrupted by another message: "I have your fucking hat."

Socrates laughed and raked the fingers of his free hand over his scalp.

"Yeah," he said to himself. "You fucking do."

He added to his message back to her, but she made him stop to read another one: "Come here now. Kiss a goddamn bus."

Wincing at his phone, he deleted all that he'd typed but never sent. Then, he typed: "No. I'm not killing myself."

He hit send, glanced at Lynnie, and saw that she wasn't interested in his search for a hat that he knew was on the head of Aspin.

Or Miley?

"Jesus."

The phone chimed again, and he read, "Then I'll start killing."

127

"No," he said quietly. "What the fuck is going on?"

"Dad?" he heard from the kitchen.

"Yeah, Lynnie?"

"That bedroom just isn't that big. Maybe it's not in there."

"Oh, uh, yeah. But my bird feeding buddy is sending some texts. I'll be back in a second."

He heard the neck of a whiskey bottle clink against a glass, and he grinned at not knowing which one it was and not caring.

Tapping quickly, he'd gotten as far as: "No. Don't. No ki—"

Her quick next message was: "Get your ass here. Bring that whiskey. I'll trade for your stupid hat. And that Miley idea."

"Okay," he wrote. "You won't come here?"

He stared at his phone, reading the message, "Lol. You just don't know do you Socrates?"

He jammed the phone into a pants pocket while looking into his stressed eyes, not able to laugh at how each one, he was certain, would be on their own, proper side of a string holding an engagement ring from long ago.

"Oh, God. Is she already here? Wendy! Rae Cat!"

Chapter 22 – Charging in with an Axe

Between quick breaths, Socrates said to his daughter, "Lynnie, I, uh, maybe left the hat in the lobby. I'm going to run down and take a look."

"Running more. Good. Alright, I'll wait here."

"Thanks."

He walked quickly through the kitchen and a few steps later, he stopped at the door, his hand on the doorknob.

"God."

"What?"

Turning, he said, "Oh, uh, nothing."

He began the short walk back into the kitchen and grabbed most of the notes off of the table, but two sheets were still in Lynnie's hand.

"What?"

"I just think I'll look these over on the way."

He stopped to hold her gaze, a squinting look that didn't change even as a smile grew.

"Seriously, Dad? Even just to run—because you're on an exercise kick—down to the lobby to look for a hat?"

"Um. I, uh, do some of my best thinking when I'm on the move."

"Fine."

She held out her two sheets.

"Wouldn't want you to run out of reading material."

He laughed and said, "No, you can keep those. This is enough to block—"

She stared, her eyebrows locked up high.

"Uh, any distractions. Distractions aren't good."

"Even in the hallway?"

Shaking his head, he said, "The stairs too."

He saw her relaxed smile and added, "The stairs can be the worst."

"Fine."

He turned and hurried back to the door, got his shields ready, and pulled in the door.

* * *

With the sheets flat, tipped sideways, and scraping under his chin, Socrates swung the door closed behind him. After maneuvering to the middle of the hallway, he faced the end of it, where the stairs lurked, waiting for him, and adjusted the notes to be sure that not a single red, orange, or yellow shape from Hell could be seen.

He started to walk, relaxing at his progress quickly bringing him to the beginning of the balcony section, where the lobby, with its multitude of twinkling suns, could all be viewed by looking beyond the railing.

Still blocking the hallway carpet, he peeked around the corner and saw Wendy and Rae on the burgundy couch. The girl was too focused on a book, but the cat, who never missed anything, didn't miss him and his papers.

"That cat . . ."

He took a step and that caught Wendy's eye. She smiled and waved up at him, so he first made sure that he was leaning out over the railing enough, then he waved the papers around.

"Very important stuff!"

She nodded and kept watching him as he resumed his trek.

At the top of the stairs, he again looked at Wendy and frowned for just a second at seeing that she was still studying him.

The cat too. Always that Rae Cat.

He waved the papers around again and said, "I'm coming. Be there in a—"

Every last sheet slipped from his hand, and he leaned over to watch them all fluttering softly to the tile floor of the lobby.

He looked up when Wendy giggled and said, "Uh-oh!"

"Oops," he said and held the railing with both hands.

Still looking over the side at the constellation of papers scattered around, he took one step, then another before looking again at the girl and her cat.

She was giggling softly with a hand over her mouth.

The cat's green eyes only stared.

"Almost there, Wendy."

He watched the papers, though they showed no signs of running off to hide, and kept taking slow, measured steps until he reached the very bottom.

Standing with his hands on his hips, taking quick breaths, Socrates said to Wendy, "That sure is kind of funny, Wendy."

She nodded as she dropped her hand and said, "We thought so!"

He smiled at her, squinted for a second at the frozen, staring black cat, then went to gather up his notes.

*   *   *

With one knee resting on the cool floor, Socrates turned his eyes toward the building entrance, the glass door that could open out to the sunshine dropping all around the shadow of the fabric awning to warm the concrete sidewalk.

Or it could show him someone who looked like Miley, who dressed like Miley, who could be Miley.

Who had just spoken of starting some killing.

"Jesus," he said softly as he reached around blindly, his fingertips finding nothing but clean tiles.

The giggling brought him back, and he looked to the couch.

Wendy was grinning and shaking her head.

Rae Cat had tipped hers, but she kept her thoughts to herself.

"Oh, Wendy, I'm so distracted today."

He quickly picked up every sheet, got them all lined up with each other in his hand, then walked to the couch.

"What about, Mr. Lewis? Feeding the birds?"

He'd already turned his head, scanning every bit of the sidewalk that could be seen. Even across the street.

"Mr. Lewis?"

"Huh?" he said, snapping his head toward her. "Oh, Wendy, it's just such a sunny day, that's all."

"It's a good day to feed the birds?"

His attention was drawn again to the outside, and there was no hooker charging in with an axe.

"You're right, Wendy. It's a perfect day for that. Maybe I can even find my—"

"Hat? You lost your hat."

He shook his head, looking down at the girl and her cat.

"I sure did," he said, pointing toward the door. "Somewhere out there."

"That's another good story, Mr. Lewis."

He pointed at her, bouncing his hand, and said, "You mean that I should write a story about my adventure out there to find my hat?"

She nodded quickly, her eyebrows high.

"Huh. That sure will be some wild kind of adventure, won't it?"

She shrugged and began petting the cat without looking at her.

"Okay," he said. "You talked me into it. I just need to get back upstairs for—"

"Birdseed!"

"Yes, Wendy. Yes!"

He got the papers in his hand ready, then aimed himself and the thin stack that promised to preserve his sanity toward the stairway.

Chapter 23 – I Look Sexy as Hell

Out of breath after running up the steps, then down the hallway to his door, all while blocking any possible view of the floor with the note papers, Socrates leaned his back into his closed apartment door.

"No hat," Lynnie said, pointing at his head.

"Oh, uh, no. It wasn't in the lobby."

"And you're exercising, which is good."

"Yeah. Yeah, I sure am."

She tipped her head and watched him breathing deeply and not leaving the door.

"Did you get some valuable studying done?"

She glanced down at the papers in his hand by his side.

"Uh, not much. No."

"Well, I can't stay much longer. Come on back to the table. We should probably figure out what we're doing about all that," she said, pointing at his notes.

He held them up, gave them a look, and said, "Alright. Yeah," and started walking toward the kitchen doorway.

His phone chirped in his pocket, and he froze mid-step. Lynnie popped her eyebrows up.

"Still with the bird guy, Dad? What's up with that guy?"

He held his hands out to both sides and said, "Lots of folks really care about those pigeons. What else can I say?"

When his phone chimed again in his pocket, he never broke his gaze with Lynnie. His smile barely showed itself, in a strained way, at the sight of her shaking her head and pointing at the source of the alerts.

"Maybe too much. Do you even know if they're hungry?"

While walking past the table toward his bedroom, he said, "Uh, no. I don't know anything about them, Lynnie."

He pushed the door mostly closed, then opened it enough to say to her, "They always eat, though. I do know that much."

Then, he pushed the door until it almost latched and read her message: "I'm coming to your bldg."

His quick message back read: "No don't!"

She wrote: "I look sexy as hell too. Wow this skirt is short. Time to meet the family."

He quietly closed his bedroom door the rest of the way, then sent: "Please no."

Staring at his phone, he waited and prayed for a response, all while his heart was beating its way out of his chest.

But there was no reply from Aspin.

"Dammit. Come on."

Nothing. Until it chimed again.

She'd sent: "I'll be there in 15."

A quick look at his left wrist, after bunching up the sleeve, brought out a heavy groan, then he repeated it to look at the wristwatch on the right side.

He started to type a reply, then grimaced in pain and shot the phone back into his pocket.

"God, she's coming. Wendy and Rae Cat really need to hide."

He swung open his bedroom door and staggered back a step, almost falling, at the shrill ringing from Lynnie's phone.

*   *   *

When Socrates got to the table, he saw Lynnie smiling and tapping her phone before she looked up at him.

"That was Mom. She—"

"Is everything alright? She's okay?"

"Yeah, Dad. Calm down. She just said that she's stopping by."

His eyes could have been small plates with dark marbles floating uneasily in the middle.

"Uh, sure. When?"

Lynnie nodded at him and said, "She said about fifteen minutes."

"Oh, God . . ."

He leaned his back into the refrigerator and a second later, he grabbed the countertop for support too.

"You don't look happy."

"Oh, no, I really am. I, uh . . ."

He looked around, squinting at everything, then back at Lynnie.

"It's just, um, kind of a mess. I should—"

"Look, Dad, I'm not dumb. I know you got this thing with keeping things neat and—"

"Yeah, but that's just it. They're not neat. Things are not at all—"

"And that's good," she said, nodding. "Mom will be proud of you. Way to go, Dad."

He covered his mouth and whispered, so low that he was sure that Lynnie couldn't hear, "Jesus."

"What, Dad? What was that?"

"Um, just clearing my throat."

Lynnie tipped her head toward the bottles.

"That'll help."

"Oh, I don't know. Not with your mother—"

"You're so out of touch. Mom likes a little of that sometimes too."

He stared at her.

She stared back, then shrugged.

Chapter 24 – She Pointed at Socrates

Lynnie hadn't yet relaxed her shrug, and Socrates blurted out, "The notes. I have to go downstairs again."

She smirked and pointed at the table.

"What the hell are you talking about? They're right there."

"No. I mean, yeah, but, uh, not all of them. I think I missed a sheet down there."

She started reaching for the papers, but he beat her to them.

"I'll just take those when I go. That way I can—"

"Make sure they're perfectly organized? Is that it?"

He stared for a second before speaking.

"Uh, yeah. Hey, I'm working on it, alright?"

"Fine, Dad. I think I'll wait in the lobby for Mom anyway. Let's reschedule sometime to go over that perfectly arranged set of notes."

"I deserve your sarcasm."

"Yep."

She started to rise up from the chair.

"No! I mean, take your time. I'm going to run on ahead."

"And you do mean 'run,' don't you?"

"Oh, yeah, Lynnie. Damn right."

"I like that you're leaving Jesus out of things lately."

"Well, he, uh, he's probably busy with more important stuff. He doesn't need me calling him all the—"

"You were never calling him."

He stared. She stared.

"Okay. You're right. It probably never made sense to call anyone by that name."

She squinted for a long moment, then said, "Huh? What a weird thing to say."

He let a deep breath flap his lips as it rushed out.

"It's just been a weird day. Okay, I'm going."

With notes in hand, he scurried into the hallway and slammed the door with a boom.

*　*　*

"Oh, sweet Jesus."

He stood with the shield in place and waited for his breaths to calm.

They didn't, so he started taking long steps toward the stairs, notes in one hand and the other dragging its nails along the wall.

Until the wall ended. Then, he grabbed the railing but didn't dare look out into the vast lobby, where he knew there were all kinds of eyes watching him.

Well, two kinds, he corrected himself.

Hooking his fingers around to keep his arm tightly connected, he kept going and the times when the edges of the papers flapped, flashing a view of the floor, he snapped his head up so quickly to stare at the ceiling that he risked breaking his own neck.

Finally, he'd arrived. The stairway.

And all of its devious purple pitfalls that were haphazardly distributed to annoy and possibly murder him.

He took the rail, pretended to read the project notes from a distance not much farther than the end of his nose, and rushed to the bottom.

Feeling like purple circles were grabbing and biting at him with every step.

*　*　*

"Hi, Mr. Lewis."

"Hello, Wendy. I'm back."

"For exercise?"

"Oh, uh, no. Not this time."

She pointed toward the door and said, "Time to feed the birds?"

"No. Soon, though. No, I just wondered if you ever get tired of sitting around down here. Isn't upstairs better sometimes?"

She shrugged and said, "Sometimes."

"Like, maybe, right now?"

She stared at him, then looked down at the cat, who had never stopped staring up at him.

"I forgot my favorite book at home."

"Oh, a favorite book. Yes, you'd probably like to have that."

She looked up at him and nodded.

But she didn't get up.

"Um,"—he looked quickly at the front door and didn't see Aspin—"that book is waiting up there. For you."

She shrugged, sighed, and said, "I know. But I like it here too."

He looked around at all of the bright colors, every furnishing and decorative piece displaying an endless variety. Then, he looked up at all of the suns that never moved. They only rested there on their own little chains, performing such cheerful work.

"It's a very nice place, Wendy. Yeah, I like it here too. But I bet it's nice in your home too."

"It's nice. But it's not the same."

"No?"

She shook her head and didn't smile.

"Well, uh, what's the big difference?"

Still not smiling, she pointed at Socrates.

And he forgot all about murderous Aspin, dressed like hooker Miley, coming to jab rusty scissors at them all.

He choked out a raspy breath.

It was either that, he knew, or a sob.

"Well, thanks, Wendy. But—"

"Rae Cat too."

He tipped his head at seeing what might be a wet sheen on the child's eyes. A quick look at Rae showed no such emotional reaction.

"She told me."

It took two big sighs before Socrates could speak.

"You and Rae are my best reason for liking this lobby, Wendy. You can tell Rae that, alright?"

The little girl grinned and said, "Mr. Lewis, she's right here. She heard you!"

Chapter 25 – The Hellish Purple Ice Broke

Socrates clutched the phone in a tight fist, standing at the bottom of the stairs, as he wiped quickly and made sure that not a single drop of a tear would be hanging under an eye for anyone to see.

Then, he sent a text to Aspin: "Please don't come here. I think I'll come to the bridge."

The reply was immediate: "You damn well better. Don't make me wait long."

"Okay," he sent.

He half turned enough to see that Wendy wasn't creeping up on him with a black cat in her arms. Then, he stared at the phone long enough to be convinced that he'd earned some sort of uneasy truce or delay, at least, with Aspin.

"Your notes, Mr. Lewis!"

He turned his head toward the burgundy couch and said, "Oh, thank you, Wendy. Yes. Very important to study."

He stowed the phone and began lifting the notes, too close to read but just right to save his heart from exploding into a spray of red droplets on purple circles.

"Dad," Lynnie said from the top of the stairway, "are you coming back up already? Did you find that lost sheet?"

"Oh, Lynnie. I, uh, made a mistake. It was already in with the others."

He lowered the papers, wincing and groaning too softly for anyone to hear but him.

Behind him, Wendy shouted, "He's studying, Lynnie!"

He sucked in a sharp breath as he looked down at the swarm of purple torments, then back up to Lynnie at the very top.

"Are you studying still?" she said. "Come on up. I'll wait."

"I, uh . . ."

"Maybe he's exercising!" said the girl with the black cat.

Socrates spun his head quickly to see Wendy grinning at him.

Rae Cat only stared.

Focusing on that first dreadful step, he lifted his right leg and quickly counted the circles to the left of where the shoe was about to land. Then, the circles on the right had to be—

"Dad, what kind of exercise is that?"

He looked up at the sound of Lynnie's laughter, and his dangling lower leg vibrated around, unsure of where to rest.

"Just one leg!" said the girl.

He dared a quick look at Wendy and saw her holding up one finger and smiling.

The circles on the right. They had to be counted. That was the first step in the process.

He laughed out loud and said, "First step. I'm funny."

"What, Dad?"

Looking up again, he winced for just a second, then ground his eyelids shut as he thudded that shoe onto the ribbon adorned with circles that might just as well have been swimming from side to side, making counting impossible and taunting him with areas that could never be—

"I don't get it," said Lynnie. "It's like . . . slow motion climbing or something?"

He looked up to see his daughter frowning down at him.

"And where's your hat?"

"The birds took it!"

He snapped around to look at Wendy, who was covering her mouth and giggling.

"That's funny," said Lynnie. "You're funny, Wendy."

While gingerly and gradually releasing his full weight onto that horribly misplaced first step, like a doomed explorer venturing out onto a thin sheet of ice, Socrates's worried eyes looked upward again.

He twisted around that foot on step one, his arms raised to his sides for balance. Then, somewhat sure that the ice wouldn't crack, sending him into some freezing nightmare purple sea, he lifted his left.

And he froze all on his own.

"Dad?"

"Uh . . ."

"Mr. Lewis? Are you okay?"

"I, um . . ."

He kept his eyes open only long enough to see Lynnie nodding toward Wendy, then he heard her say, "He's just trying to be funny, Wendy."

"He's real funny, Lynnie!"

"Oh, Wendy, he sure—"

The hellish purple ice broke.

*   *   *

His right leg drove through the crackling ice, all the way to his knee.

On the way into the bottomless carpet ocean, his left foot, raised and ready to attempt step two, didn't have to move at all.

It slammed into the ice, cracked it like the sound of a gunshot, then pulled him down until his outstretched arms saved him, his elbows striking near the ends of a single stair runner.

"Oh, sweet Jesus. It had to happen eventually!"

He looked to his left, noted the cluster of purple circles crowding around that elbow, then attempted the same with the right side.

It was too much motion, and another gunshot filled the lobby.

"No! I can't die here on these damned steps!"

He heard a squeaky voice to his left that said, "Sure you can!"

Looking quickly, he saw only pale purple things moving, arranging themselves.

A taunting voice to his right called to him.

"And you will!"

He looked, but the sight was the same. Purple circles. Moving. Not talking.

A voice from the top of the ice stairs: "That's really funny!"

He snapped his eyes up there, recognizing Lynnie's voice, but it wasn't Lynnie.

It was an oblong purple shape, undulating like a squishy water balloon. Only a perfectly round purple circle opened and closed robotically as it continued with a goading purple accent.

"You're really a funny guy!"

How do I calculate the area of that? he wondered. There's no formula for that! And besides, it keeps moving and sloshing around!

A voice to his left, cherubic and cheerful, said, "You're making me laugh!"

He looked and was sorry that he had. A single, tiny purple circle was bouncing around, its tinier purple circle eyes blinking rapidly.

Almost hypnotized at the sight, recognizing that it was Wendy's voice, he said, "But I . . . I mean—"

He felt it more than he saw it: something watching him from the right end of the runner, so he whipped his head around.

And seeing it helped not at all.

Another purple circle was rocking from side to side, silently.

It had green eyes. And they didn't blink at all.

"God, no! This can't be happening! It's just a goddamn stairway!"

The stairway ice field gave way, all of it at once, and the purple hues didn't just race past him—he felt them daggering and knifing and spearing through him from bottom to top as he sank and sank and . . .

* * *

Socrates felt his left shoe gently touch down on a soft, carpeted surface.

He heard a voice from above, probably that oblong purple daughter, he thought, so he looked.

She wasn't oblong. Or purple.

Just his daughter.

And she was looking toward Wendy on the burgundy couch.

"One step at a time isn't enough, is it, Wendy?"

He didn't have to look. He knew that the girl was grinning and shaking her head.

And that cat. Rae Cat. All she was doing was staring.

He heard Wendy's voice.

"He has to run. He has to exercise."

She's right, he thought. Before the ice breaks again!

Still looking at the smiling face of his daughter an infinite number of steps above him, all teeming with treacherous purple creatures, Socrates ran.

He pounded each step, his breaths heavy and quick.

Until Lynnie squealed and laughed and jumped out of his way.

Someone had moved that wall closer, he thought, as he slapped both of his forearms against it to stop his dash to safety.

"Dad, you're hilarious sometimes!"

Keeping one hand welded to the wall, Socrates turned toward her, but he kept his eyes closed.

"Lynnie, this is funny too. Let's pretend my eyes are tired, so you have to help me back to my place."

"What? Seriously?"

"Sure. Here,"—he waved his free hand around, sometimes near her, sometimes not—"it's up to you."

"Well, alright," she said, still laughing.

She took his hand, and they began the walk along the balcony railing.

"Wendy's waving to you, Dad."

"Oh. Wendy."

He shook around the hand that Lynnie was holding.

"Wave my hand at her."

"You can't be serious."

"It'll make her laugh."

He felt his hand being raised, then shaken, then he heard Wendy squealing over the rail, down below on his favorite couch in the world.

"You were right. She did like that. That cat, though . . ."

"Nothing?"

"Just green eyes. Come on, blind man. Time to go home."

They took several more steps, and he dragged his free hand along the wall.

"It should be right about,"—his fingers made contact with a decorative piece mounted to the wall—"right here."

"That mask?"

"Yeah."

He felt around its features, then poked a finger into each of its open eye sockets.

"Geez, Dad. Glad I wasn't standing there."

"You can be pretty funny, too, Lynnie."

"I, uh, wasn't joking."

Chapter 26 – I Should Just Laugh?

"Okay, you got it?" she said as she placed his hand on the doorknob.

He gave it a turn, rattling it, then pushed it in.

"Whew. Yeah, thanks."

"Alright, then, I'm going to get—"

"I have to leave again, too, but can you come back inside for a minute?"

He held the door cracked open, facing it, his nose almost touching it.

"Uh, sure, Dad. What's going on?"

He gave the door a push, it squealed in, and he stepped in, too, opening his eyes as he turned back toward Lynnie.

But he held his hand up near his face, pretending to be scratching an itch. She squinted at the sight of it, then looked at his eyes.

"I have something to confess."

"I'm intrigued."

She stepped inside and closed the door behind her.

"About what?"

"About how I'm not funny at all."

"You're too modest. I just watched you—"

"That wasn't what you thought. Come on."

He turned toward the kitchen, but she grabbed his arm.

"You weren't being funny?"

"No, Lynnie, even if it *was* funny. A quick drink? It'll help."

"Me?"

"Maybe. Mostly me, though."

"Sure."

* * *

"Old or new?"

"I don't think it matters," she said and pushed her glass across the table toward him.

He nudged it until it was lined up with his, then he picked up both whiskey bottles and poured them at the same time, each glass halfway. Then, he switched the bottles and topped them off.

"You're always that fair with things?"

"Oh, uh, Lynnie. That has nothing to do with being fair. Look."

He pointed at the two seed containers which sat to his left and her right, backed up against the edge of the small round table beneath a light fixture with only two out of four bulbs lit.

She leaned to get a better view, then sat up and reached for her glass.

"Perfectly even. Oh."

"Yeah."

He lifted his glass and held it in her direction until she clinked it with hers. They both took a sip.

"Alright," she said, "you say you're not funny. Not on the stairs?"

She waited, and he shook his head.

"Alright," she said. "Maybe not in the hallway either?"

Another few shakes with his eyes flaring open briefly.

"So, what's the deal with the stairs?"

He cleared his throat, then said, "You've seen them, right? You've looked at them?"

"Uh, I haven't been crawling up and down on my hands and knees, exactly, but yeah."

"Purple . . . circles."

"I remember purple. Yeah, the steps are purple."

"Purple circles, Lynnie. They're about the biggest problem that ever—"

"Hey. Dad. Easy, alright? What about them?"

He wiped across his face several times with a sweaty palm.

"They're a stubborn bunch. It's almost impossible to step in just the right place with all of that going on."

"Uh, the 'right place' is just if you don't trip and break your neck, right?"

"Oh, no, Lynnie. Nothing's that easy. I need to step in the exact place where there are the same number of those damn circles on each side of my shoe. It's just me, though. I'd never expect you to—"

"Don't worry. I'll step wherever I damn well please."

"Good. Keep doing that. But me? It used to be just going up but now, it's going back down too. I need to get it right so that—"

"You split them up."

She pointed and grinned.

"Hey, like the seed?"

"Yeah. But I could probably do it if there wasn't some other monstrous problem with all those damn—"

"Dad! Alright, what else?"

"Each of those damn things has an area, and I have to—"

"You have to?"

"Yes! Dammit, I have to calculate all the areas of all of them, add them up for each side, then pray like hell that—"

"You seriously pray about that?"

"Uh . . . no. I, uh, wouldn't know what to pray for. I think."

"Okay, but you try to figure all that out? While you're running up or down those stairs?"

"No, not when I'm running! If I hold my breath and run, then I—"

"Make that girl think you're exercising."

"Uh, yeah."

"And that cat too."

"I don't know what that cat thinks about anything."

"No one does. So, what happened just now?"

"Those damn things swallowed me up, and I fell into them, and they were kind of laughing and kind of of—"

She grabbed his arm and said, "Dad! None of that happened."

He squinted at her for a second, then said, "No?"

She laughed and said, "Now, see? This is funny."

"I'm not being funny."

She stopped laughing.

"Then, it's not funny at all."

"There's more that's not funny."

"The hallway too?" she said.

He nodded.

"Have you seen—"

His phone chirped in his pocket, so he got it out, tapped it, and frowned while reading Aspin's message: "Where the fuck are you?"

He tapped and sent: "Coming!" then tucked the phone away and looked at his daughter.

She pointed at the seed containers and raised her eyebrows.

He shrugged and grinned.

"Bird feeding people. Go figure."

"Okay," she said, "what about the hallway?"

"Kind of the same things as the stairs. But the hallway's got all these devious red, and—"

"They're devious?"

He stared for a few seconds before saying, "Uh, okay. Maybe not devious. But it's got a bunch of red, orange, and yellow shapes all along the entire blasted length of the damn carpet in the goddamn—"

"Whoa! Dad! Easy, alright? Let me guess: you try to do some of that same nonsense in the hallway too?"

He puffed up his cheeks and let it dribble out.

"Yeah. It's impossible."

"Well, yeah. What do you expect?"

He held her steady gaze for a few seconds, then winced and said, "I guess I'm expecting too much?"

She pointed and said, "Bingo."

His lips quivered, and he couldn't speak for a moment.

"Uh, bingo? You said—"

"Yeah. So, if you—"

His phone yelled again for his attention, and he let it carry on while only gazing back at Lynnie.

She tipped her head toward the perfectly even seed containers.

He smirked and shook his head, then shrugged.

The phone got quiet.

"Well, Dad, thanks for being so open about all of that. I can sympathize."

"You can?"

"Sure. We all have our quirks. I know you didn't ask, but I won't tell Mom about any of that."

"Thanks, Lynnie."

"I do have one suggestion, though."

"What's that?"

"Get a new apartment. Try for something on the first floor."

He grinned, saying, "I'm surprised I never even thought of that."

* * *

Before opening the door to let Lynnie go first, Socrates said, "Hey, uh, feel like setting something up for me?"

"Like what?"

"Instead of your mom dropping by,"—he grimaced at his wristwatch—"maybe she and I could plan just having dinner sometime."

Her eyes got big, and a smile quickly followed.

"Really? You want to have a dinner date?"

"Well, I didn't exactly call it a—"

"Fine, Dad. Call it whatever you want."

She whipped out her phone and tapped furiously for a few seconds, then held it down, waiting and looking at Socrates.

She tipped her head from side to side, rhythmically, keeping a steady pace.

"You're good at that."

"Thanks. You wouldn't believe how many times I—"
Her phone rang, she tapped it, and a bigger smile spread.
She put it away while meeting his gaze again.
"You're on. Tomorrow at 5:00."
He blew out a deep breath and said, "Good. Yeah. So, she's not coming here right now, right?"
"Don't look so panicked, alright? Damn. No, you're on for dinner tomorrow instead."
"Thanks. Why don't you, um, go on ahead first?"
Laughing, she said, "Right, so I don't see you fall into the stairs?"
"Damn purple circles. Not that damn hallway either."
"Right, Dad. The black, blue, and green—"
"What? No! Red, orange, and yellow."
"Whatever."
"You'd care more if they were trying to kill you."
She shook her head, squinting at him.
"Yeah, they're deadly. Alright, it's been fun. We're still on for that project someday?"
"Yeah, Lynnie. And thanks."
"For?"
"Listening."
"Hey, it was your whiskey. What the hell."
"I'll take that."
"Your hat."
"My hat?"
"Better find it before dinner tomorrow. Oh, and Dad?"
"Yeah?"
"Laughing about the damn stairs and hallway helped. I could tell."
"You're saying I should just laugh at those purple circles?"
"Yeah. And the hallway's plaid and striped and paisley—"
He laughed loudly, stopping her, then said, "You made me laugh just now. On purpose."
"Try it yourself next time. Got to go."

Chapter 27 – I Still Don't Know

"She's right," he said as he stared at the man in the mirror, who was standing up straight and tall. "I have to get that hat back."

He'd just started to pick at where the tape had held the string to the top part of the mirror's frame when his phone chirped.

He tapped it and read Aspin's text: "Now. Or I can throw this damn hat off the bridge."

"No," he typed, "don't! I'm coming!"

He hit send, then stared at the phone. But it had no more to say.

Looking again at his own eyes, he leaned to the left, then to the right, then back to straight up.

"Huh. That got fixed. Those damn animals too. God."

Just his eyes got tipped down to look at the rummage sale table appearance of his dresser top.

"Jesus, if I could just straighten that out some."

He spun first to his right, then back around to his left, surveying his room.

"What if she wants to come see this dump?"

He faced the mirror again and got out the ring, which was warm from hanging from a white shoestring under his shirt.

"What if she wants this offered a second time?"

It felt cooler when he let it drop back inside.

"First, I have to get that hat. That means seeing Aspin."

He winced at his reflection.

"Or Miley. Jesus, I still don't know. Should I go see whoever that is?"

He turned to leave the room, then jerked himself back around, his eyes looking everywhere in the clutter of clothes and stray birdseeds.

He zeroed in on the gum and grabbed it.

"And talking to myself. God, wasn't I going to stop that?"

Chapter 28 – Not Always Somebody's Fault

Sweating, out of breath, wearing a trench coat but no fedora, Socrates looked down at Wendy and Rae Cat.

"You laughed all the way, Mr. Lewis."

"I sure did. It's a, um, different kind of exercise thing."

"It's funny. Are you going to feed the birds?"

He reached into his coat pockets and shook the coat around from in there.

"No seed. Not this time."

"You still don't have your hat?"

"No. But I think I know where it is."

"Where?"

"On a bridge where I was walking before. If it didn't blow over the side. Hey, weren't you going to go home for a while?"

She shrugged and said, "I did, but my mom chased me out."

"Why?"

She shrugged again.

"She said she wanted to vacuum."

"Oh. And I bet Rae Cat doesn't like that?"

With a solemn face, the girl shook her head, so Socrates looked into the cat's green eyes.

"You don't like that, Rae Cat?"

Nothing but a stare. Not even a blink.

"Huh. Nothing to say."

"She's very quiet all the time."

"If Rae Cat gets scared of the vacuum cleaner, is that your mom's fault?"

"I don't think so. Uh-uh."

"I don't think so either. Why don't you think so?"

Wendy shrugged, then said, "She's not trying to scare Rae. She's just cleaning up."

"So, if something happens that Rae Cat doesn't like, that's not always somebody's fault."

She scrunched up her face, then said, "I don't know. I don't think so, Mr. Lewis."

Quick footsteps down the stairs caused them both to look at Rosa halfway down, smiling and waving.

"Hi, Mom!"

"Hello, Wendy. Hello, Socrates."

"Hi, Rosa. Wendy has been keeping me company before I run out for some errands."

"He has to find his hat, Mom."

She was already close to Socrates, but she took another step and gave an exaggerated look at the top of his head.

And he noticed her deep inhaling as she sampled the air all around him.

"Well, no hat there. That's true."

She looked him in the eye and said, "Really, I like that I don't notice a thing."

He smiled at her, and Wendy said, "That's because it's on the bridge, Mom."

She looked at her daughter, then back to Socrates and said, "Oh, a hat on a bridge. That's something."

"If it's still there," he said. "I should run. It was—"

Wendy said, "He's going to run. He means it."

"Oh, Rosa, I've just been, um, running up the—"

"Down, too, Mr. Lewis," said Wendy.

"Yes, she's right. Up and down. Trying to exercise a little."

"That's very commendable," she said, nodding.

To Wendy, she said, "Isn't that very commendable, Honey? Who knew that Mr. Lewis was such an inspiration?"

"Funny too," Wendy said.

"Oh?" Rosa said, looking at him with her eyebrows up.

"Oh, uh, it was nothing. Just a little fun the last time I traveled up the steps."

"And the hallway!" she said with a giggle.

"Yes, the hallway too. Wendy has a wonderful laugh. I like hearing that."

Rosa tipped her head toward the couch and said, "Not like that cat. She doesn't make a peep."

"Cats don't peep, Mom."

Rosa never looked at Wendy, just rolled her eyes for Socrates, who grinned back at her.

"I really better go."

"For that hat," said Wendy.

"Yes. Have a good afternoon, Rosa. You too, Wendy and Rae Cat."

They all said their goodbyes, except for the cat, and Socrates took the ten or so steps to the building's door, pushed it out, then stopped and took out his phone.

To Aspin, he sent: "On my way."

Chapter 29 – Starting It All Over

Standing at the highest point of the bridge, Socrates looked out over the deserted train tracks that had appeared so desolate without a coat of sunshine. He reached up to adjust the brim of his hat.

"God. I know it's not there."

He looked to the far side at the nearly bumper-to-bumper traffic moving along quickly on the cross street. It took only a few seconds before he saw the first bus race past, then roll itself out of sight behind tall brick buildings.

"Jesus. Buses."

He held a hand up again not for the brim but to shield his eyes, giving him a more conclusive opinion that Aspin was waiting for him.

Just about where Miley had died.

Unless that *was* Miley.

"God, this is ridiculous."

He leaned his back against the rail and watched the slower vehicles on the bridge crawl past, and he laughed, glad that he had.

Because a police car was about to pass him, and he kept the bottle, and his hand on that bottle, inside his coat until it had passed.

Still watching it, he got out the whiskey, turned toward the railroad valley to uncap it, then took a quick drink.

"That helps. Don't need any goddamn gum out here either. Huh."

With the bottle safely packed away, he began his walk toward Aspin, but he caught his breath and stopped.

"No," he said at the sound of scraping over the side. "It has to be a broken sign again."

The scraping got louder.

He stepped closer, then put both hands on the railing.

Which he promptly let go to take a few steps back.

"I'm not even looking."

Glaring up at the sky, he yelled, "I'm done with monsters trying to eat me. Done!"

No monsters disagreed with him.

Someone in a passing car did offer a comment, though.

"Go ahead and jump, psycho!"

He didn't bother to look, but he heard the laughter fading into the rumble of traffic.

*　*　*

Walking toward her, his eyes got stuck on her legs. The skirt was short, the heels high, and Miley's cheap, fake fur jacket gave him a shiver in the warm sunshine.

As she faced away, toward the street teeming with fast traffic, he couldn't shake the certainty that he would soon see Miley again.

She'd tell him that it had all been a clever hoax. Some kind of illusion.

No bus had hit her and carried her away like trash in a flooded gutter.

That there never was any twin named Aspin. Never any twin at all.

But Miley's head began to turn before her legs, then she stepped enough to face him as he approached after his hike over the bridge.

Socrates prepared himself to face an angry, homicidal glare because there was a chance that the hooker standing there was really Aspin.

But the pleasant smile was that of Miley.

She waved, and even that gesture carried the mannerisms of Miley.

He'd gotten close enough to see the blue of her eyes, which called out to him even against a backdrop built of normal city colors, not gray and dark and damp from endless rains.

"Miley?"

Her smile lessened, and she tipped her head, and his hat, slightly.

"Who did you expect?"

"But you . . . I thought—"

"You went and stole my notebook, didn't you?"

"Yeah, sorry, but you were already—"

"You really think I'd be mad that you took my notes?"

"No, because you . . . I mean, I only—"

"Hey, I told you about them, remember?"

"Yeah, you did. It was like a diary, you said. A streetwalker's diary. I'd call it a philosopher's diary."

She scoffed and said, "Something a lunatic would do."

"Lunatic? But you couldn't have known that Miley said that . . . if you're not really—"

"You think too much, Socrates. Lunatic is a common word. Did you read all of it?"

He'd moved to stand beside her, both facing vehicle traffic while people traffic shuffled past behind them.

"Uh, just once. Quickly. I need to go back and—"

"It's not all in there," she said, then tapped her temple. "Some bits are only up here."

"Uh, like drill bits?"

She shrugged while gazing back at him.

"Sure. Maybe."

He stared at her without answering, then blurted out, "But I saw you—"

"Doing all kinds of crazy shit. Yeah. That was fun, wasn't it? Out in the rain all night?"

She tipped her eyes up, then lifted his hat with both hands.

"So sweet of you to loan me this."

He started to reach for it, but she set it back down, then brushed her hair back over her shoulders.

"Here's something that I didn't write down. Just think about it, alright?"

"Okay. We really have to talk about that stuff right now?"

"It leads to something. You'll see. Ready?"

"If you want. Okay."

"Look around."

He listened to her as they both looked across the street, above the rolling cars and trucks at the brick buildings, then at the blue skies resting above them.

"Big things and small things. Complicated and simple. Things no one can explain. How did it all get here? How does it all stay here?"

"Uh, it just . . . I mean, it all—"

"You know the truth when you slow down and look. Really look. Stop lying to yourself—you see proof of God everywhere."

He turned to her first, then she turned enough to hold his gaze.

"Tell me, Socrates: where do you see Jesus in any of this?"

He didn't look around again, just shook his head softly.

"Uh, nowhere. Just in a book."

She grinned and pointed at him, then said, "In someone's words. So, you'd have to have faith."

"Faith in Jesus?"

"Yeah, but first? Faith in a book."

"So," he said, "Jesus is just . . . a crosswind?"

She shrugged and said, "Sure could be."

He never blinked, staring into her serious blue eyes.

"Eh," she said, then looked away, "enough of that."

"Enough about God?"

She turned back to him and said, "Yep. Do you like me?"

His lips fumbled and faltered, then he got everything working and said, with a grin, "Uh, I think I want to know who you are."

Her lips sagged from a smile into the beginning of a frown, and she pointed at him again.

"I can tell you that I was messing with you just now, but you'll still think I'm Miley."

"I, um . . ."

"Almost the same to have her twin, huh?"

"Jesus," he said, "who the hell are you? Come on already."

The frown worsened, relaxing only enough for her to smirk.

"Says the man who doesn't even remember his own name."

"I remember it! I just—"

"So, is Socrates the twin of whatever the hell your real name is?"

He stared, squinting at her as she waited.

"My . . . my twin?"

"You were born into evil. All of us were. You seem to think you can get yourself across this sea of evil just by changing your name—starting it all over."

"Aspin, I don't—"

"Fucking pay attention. I'm going to explain why you killed Miley."

"I didn't kill any—"

"Listen to me, goddammit. This is Miley the hooker's idea, but she didn't get to write it down because you killed her before she—"

"No, I never—"

"Just shut the fuck up, already!"

He looked around quickly at a lot of faces staring at what looked like a deranged hooker yelling at a customer on a busy sidewalk.

"God. Easy, alright?"

She grinned and in a calm voice said, "Sure. Why not?"

A few seconds passed as she demonstrated her sudden calm.

"Miley was more of a scholar than you ever will be, self-called Socrates. She probably listed some names for Satan, right?"

"Uh, the Old Serpent. She said that."

She scoffed and said, "Yeah, so you said. Alright, well, supposedly the devil's got this thing where he masquerades as being full of bright light. A Mr. Innocence kind of thing. He lies. That's a big lie, and there's not a damn thing good about him."

"Uh, okay. He's a liar."

"Yep. Miley showed me some videos on her phone, which got pulverized by that goddamn bus just like every bone in—"

"Hey, come on! Just tell me."

"Sure. You can probably find the videos somewhere anyway. It's about the moment of conception. When a sperm cell gets chummy with an egg, what do you see?"

"Uh, I saw that once. The video of . . ."

His mouth slacked open as he stared at her blue eyes.

"Oh, God. No way."

"Yeah. A flash of light."

"That's from the Old Serpent?"

"He almost sounds fun when you call him that. Like a jolly old inhabitant of some reptile park, just basking under a heat—"

"Forget that! You're saying that Satan is involved with conception? For all of us?"

"More like Lucifer. Sure makes you wonder, huh? Isn't this supposed to be his world, Socrates? He's right there to help welcome each of us into his fucking kingdom."

"No, that can't be. I don't—"

"It gets worse. Sure you want to hear?"

"Yeah, I'm sure."

"Are you fucking sure, Socrates?"

"Jesus, yeah. Yeah, I'm sure."

"You like sex?"

He scoffed and looked away, shaking his head.

"Focus, dammit. Look at my legs."

He didn't hesitate.

"You looking at the hooker's legs?"

"Yeah. Yeah, I am."

"And you're liking what you see. Now, I'll ask you again: do you like sex?"

He groaned and looked out at the traffic.

"Aspin, of course, like most folks, I—"

"What a rush of pleasure, huh? Almost like it's some kind of magic?"

He turned back to her, meeting her bright blue glare.

"What is seduction?" she said. "Why do you suppose that's so strong? Like hardly anyone can fucking resist it?"

"Uh, magic?"

"Dark magic, Socrates. Dark sex magic, probably like it's summoning Lucifer with his goddamn flash of fake bullshit light to drag us all screaming into this fucking place."

"Screaming? That's why—"

"Day one, long before you can feel anything else, you feel evil getting burned into you. Might as well fucking scream when you finally pop out."

"Miley put that all together? She figured that—"

"Listen. Think about how much evil revolves around sex. Maybe that's why Miley felt like she was damned and she had to escape that life any way she could. That fucking crosswind just pushed her over the edge. She needed to get across a sea of evil too."

"She did kind of say that."

"She did it the only way she could."

"So, she thought sex was all twisted up with magic spells?"

"Yeah, maybe it's all dark fucking magic spells, if you'll pardon the pun."

He laughed shakily and said, "That's a good fucking pun."

"Thanks. Are you starting to get what they mean by 'original sin?'"

"Oh, shit. Goddammit. So, what do we do?"

"We? The world can go fuck itself. All I care about right now is you."

Her eyes narrowed into tight slits, thin slices of blue scalding his eyes.

"You're evil. You killed Miley. Now, get in the fucking road and kill your own goddamn self."

*　*　*

Aspin's thin lines of accusatory blue never left Socrates's eyes as she pivoted to get between him and the sidewalk. He almost fell off of the curb as he turned to face her, his back to a line of parked cars and the first murdering lane beyond them.

"I don't—"

She shoved him with both hands, bending him back before he stepped down from the curb with one leg.

"You fucking killed her."

She shoved him again, and he backed until he was halfway along the width of the parked cars to each side of him.

"I didn't want her to die! Dammit, Aspin!"

She closed the distance, and he raised both hands, palms toward her.

"Evil. You were born fucking evil."

Her hands were up, ready to push him again, and he gave a quick glance to each side and saw that he could take another step without getting butchered.

He took that step.

She took another one too.

"Dammit, I'm not evil! I didn't want Miley to—"

"Did you grab her? You're big and strong, you drunk son of a bitch. Did you just lift her up and drag her away from the goddamn bus?"

"No. I tried once, but she—"

She shoved him again, and he saw that he was right at the edge of the parked vehicles. One more step and he'd become a bag of meat baiting a bus.

Aspin closed in on him again, eyes like blue fire, hands ready for the final push.

"Why the fuck didn't you? Why didn't you save her, you evil fucking bastard?"

He felt the wind from the zipping cars whipping his coat each time one passed. And there was no need to look to his right as a loud rumble identified what was speeding his way.

Glaring at him, their faces close, she lifted his hat with both hands and placed it on his head. She held the brim and smoothed it a couple of times, and she didn't let it go.

"You ready to die with your goddamn hat?"

"Uh, I don't want to die."

"Did she?"

The bus's grumbling had become a roar. The driver gave one very quick toot of the horn.

"I don't know," he said, pleading. "Maybe?"

He shook with one deep exhale, then looked calmly into her eyes.

"But Aspin, Miley had free will."

Her eyes relaxed, and he stared into two pools of blue, cool ponds that were there to soothe him at the time of his death.

She dropped her hands to his chest, and he still looked only into her eyes, even though just a nudge would mean his end.

When he felt her hands sliding up, maybe to his throat, he leaned back, into the traffic lane without taking a step.

But she didn't push him. She rested her hands on his shoulders.

"I had to respect that," he said. "Her wishes mattered."

She held him gently and tipped him back toward her, until they were so close that they could rub noses.

"She wasn't a piece of trash," he said.

He saw a soft sheen on her eyes and if there was still any anger there, he failed to see it.

He said, "Dammit, I should have just held her."

She pulled him closer, dropped her hands down to wrap around his waist, and rested her head on his shoulder.

Her breath warmed his neck.

"Why?" she said, her voice breaking. "Tell me why."

Three quick toots on a horn preceded a hurricane gust as the bus howled past them, fluttering his coat, flapping his fedora onto the car beside them, and caressing his face with her hair.

"Because . . . I loved her."

* * *

Her sobbing shook them both, and he stared back at the few stragglers still watching from the sidewalk behind Aspin.

"Of course," she said. "You had no choice but to love her."

"I, uh, think I know why, at least part of it."

He paused, but she only held him and kept her head on his shoulder, her nose warmed by the skin of his neck.

"Uh, hookers and philosophy," he said. "It's like she was made for me."

Her single laugh shook him, too, but he smiled at it that time.

Her arms still around him, she leaned back to look at him, and he saw a thin wet path on each cheek.

"About time you admitted that to yourself."

"Oh, about hookers and—"

"No. How you felt about her."

"Oh, that. Yeah. Did I just admit it to Miley too?"

She smiled softly, blue eyes catching some of the sunlight, but she didn't say anything.

He stared at her lips for a moment, then said, "Jesus."

Still close but speaking loudly enough to be heard over the traffic, she said, "I have a confession too."

"About . . ."

"It's my fault Miley had to die."

"What? You weren't even there."

She looked down but didn't let him go.

"That priest came to me first with that goddamn crosswind bullshit. Miley was in the next room, sick and stoned out of her mind."

"You were with her then?"

"We were never far apart. Never."

She looked up, and he saw fresh moisture that helped to sparkle the blue of her eyes.

"I saw the fucking trap right away, and I told that son of a bitch to go tell Miley about it. Told that thing that I wasn't the type that would care about that bullshit. Not me."

"So—"

"So, it did. The damn thing told her instead."

She squeezed her eyes shut, and a single tear from each one twisted along the paths already clinging to her cheeks.

"It's my fault she's dead, Socrates. My goddamn fault."

"No, no, that can't—"

She placed a fingertip against his lips.

"We have some things in common, you and I," she said.

His lips still didn't have her permission to let him speak, so he tipped his head and waited.

"We're both to blame for there being no more Miley," she said.

She took her finger away and leaned back from him.

The traffic, vehicular and pedestrian, hurried past the couple embracing between parked cars.

"Aspin, I—"

She shook her head and wiped her cheeks gently.

"Is that who I am?"

She released him and took a few steps backwards.

"Oh, Jesus."

"No. That's not my name."

"No, I mean . . . Miley?"

She shook her head and said, "You saw Miley die, didn't you?"

"God, I sure did. That goddamn bus—"

"Socrates."

He froze in the sunlight.

"What?"

"You saw a lot of giant animals, too, didn't you?"

"I, uh, yeah, they were—"

"And did *they* really happen?"

His lips quivered uselessly, and she tipped her head and gazed into his eyes. Two delicate doors opened and closed slowly, teasing him with the perfect shade of blue.

"No," he said in almost a whisper. "Those animals . . . didn't happen."

He stared at her lips as they formed just the beginning of a smile.

"It seems your life is just full of illusions, hmm?"

She spun herself around and began a slow strut away from him.

"Oh, dear Jesus," he said to himself as he watched the breezes sweeping her hair all across Miley's fake fur jacket.

She stopped after only a few steps, shook her hair to one side, and turned enough to again show him eyes of blue against a city that had no colors to compete.

She tipped her head toward her destination and said, "Choose one illusion . . . then make it real."

Without allowing him even a second to respond, she resumed her easy stride, swaying her hips and hair, and with a drum pounding in his chest, he gazed at her as she began to blend with people walking in both directions.

"Sweet God almighty."

He took one step, then stopped for his hat, still waiting on the parked car. Just as he reached for it, the roaring and horn blasting and wind gusts from another bus lofted it out of his reach.

He half-climbed onto the car, grabbed the hat, and put it on crooked, then turned quickly and took a few steps up onto the sidewalk.

Aspin had vanished into the crowds.

"Jesus, like an illusion."

He ignored the staring eyes all around him as he began a quick walk toward his apartment, in the opposite direction that she'd taken.

But he stopped after only a few steps.

He reached into his shirt and brought out the engagement ring.

After a moment of looking down at it playing with the sunlight, as shining and hopeful as when he'd bought it, a smile took hold.

And he turned to look back the other way.

"Miley."

About the Author

Edward Allen Karr was born, raised, and continues to reside in Ohio, USA. His adult life has followed a meandering path, ranging from working an automotive assembly line to designing space flight hardware. And through all of it, he's seen that life is a captivating and ultimately unexplainable endeavor. His writing seeks to add a splash of wonder to a world already awash in it.

For more about Edward Allen Karr and his writing, visit
LakesideLetters.com

* * *